Note to Readers

While the Allertons and Moes are fictional families, the choices they face are typical of life in 1927. The Roaring Twenties was a time of wild parties and music. Young people had lived through the seriousness of World War I and the fear of the flu epidemic. They wanted to enjoy life.

Many of them, like Addy's friends in this book, had lost either one or both parents to the war and the flu outbreak. Sometimes the adults who took over caring for these orphans let them do things that weren't good for them.

Also, because Prohibition made the sale and consumption of alcoholic beverages illegal, bootleggers began smuggling moonshine and other liquor to cities and towns. Gangsters made huge amounts of money through this illegal activity.

Great strides in the development of airplanes were made during the twenties as well. When Charles Lindbergh flew *The Spirit of St. Louis* nonstop across the Atlantic Ocean in May 1927, people throughout the world celebrated. Transatlantic flight was still risky, however. When Lindbergh was ready to return to the United States from France, he and his plane traveled by ship.

The
BOOTLEGGER
MENACE

Bonnie Hinman

PUBLISHING, INC.
Uhrichsville, Ohio

To Donna Boyd and our fourth- and fifth-grade Sunday school classes in Joplin, Missouri. Thanks for all the good ideas and support.

© MCMXCVIII by Barbour Publishing, Inc.

ISBN 1-57748-454-1

Published by Barbour Publishing, Inc.
P.O. Box 719
Uhrichsville, Ohio 44683
http://www.barbourbooks.com

ecpa Member of the
Evangelical Christian
Publishers Association

Printed in the United States of America.

Cover illustration by Peter Pagano.
Inside illustrations by Adam Wallenta.

CHAPTER 1

Exciting News

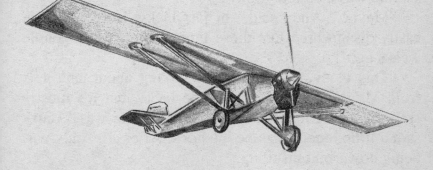

Harry braked his bike to a stop in front of Addy's house. He flung the bike up against the fence and burst through the wire gate that opened into his cousin's front yard. Addy sat on the porch, curled up in a chair, with a tablet and pencil in her lap.

"Addy!" Harry yelled as he ran up the sidewalk. "Have you heard about Lindbergh's flight? Isn't it the most exciting thing ever?"

Addy put her feet down and sat up straight. "What on earth are you talking about? What exciting thing?"

"Charles Lindbergh's flight. He flew his airplane all

alone from New York City to Paris. He's the first pilot to do that."

"All that way by himself? How long did it take?"

"Over thirty-three hours." Harry climbed the steps to sink down on a small stool that was near Addy.

"I don't see how that's possible. A person couldn't stay awake that long just sitting in a seat."

"I don't know how he did it, but he had to stay awake to keep on the right course," Harry said. "The newspaper said he was incredibly brave."

"Maybe," Addy said, "or just lucky. He could have easily disappeared like those French fliers did a couple weeks ago."

"This is an American we're talking about, and he's from Minnesota, too. He may be lucky, but it's mostly skill. He's probably the best pilot there ever was," Harry said a little louder than he intended. After all, Addy was being downright insulting.

"Oh, settle down," she said with a grin, "and quiet down. I'm waiting for a phone call." She glanced through the screen door toward the telephone table that sat in the front hall. "Whether he's brave or foolhardy, at least he got to do something exciting and new." Her face sobered. "That's lucky."

"What do you mean?" Harry asked. "You sound like something's wrong and, anyhow, where were you at church this morning?" Usually he and Addy sat side by side during church services and managed to hold whispered conversations between hymns or write notes during church business reports. "Were you sick?"

"Not really," Addy replied and twisted a brown curl around her finger. "I was extra tired, that's all. I didn't get to bed very early last night."

"Why?" Harry persisted. He had never heard his cousin say she was tired before. She was kind of quiet and a little shy, but she always had plenty of energy. Besides, her parents were strict about bedtimes and mealtimes and just about everything else.

"You ask too many questions," Addy said flatly. "I went with a friend to a play, and we were late getting home."

"What friend?"

"I can't see that it's any business of yours," Addy said. "I do have friends, you know, in spite of leading a totally boring life." She jumped up, dumping her tablet and paper to the porch floor.

"You're sure cross," Harry said. "I was just wondering, that's all. Anyhow, I came over here to see what you thought about Lindbergh's flight and see if you wanted to ride bikes downtown to get some different newspapers. It would be fun to read what all the other papers are saying— besides your father's paper, that is. But you don't seem very interested."

"I am interested, but I have other things on my mind," Addy said.

"What could be more important than Lindbergh's flight? It's the triumph of man over nature, or at least that's what the radio man said." Harry was going to continue talking about his favorite subject, but just then he noticed that Addy was frowning.

"Harry, there are tons of things that are more important

to me. Such as being treated like a baby by my parents. They act like I'm four instead of fourteen." Addy paced the length of the porch. "They make me wear this horrible dress." She gestured at her navy blue dress. "And I'm the only girl in Minneapolis who doesn't have her hair bobbed."

"I think you look nice," Harry said tentatively. He wasn't sure that this was the right time to say something.

"Well, thanks, I guess, but I want to look more modern. Susan says that I could look way older with some different clothes. And Barrett says I'd be the bee's knees with bobbed hair. After all, these are the twenties."

"Are they your new friends?"

Addy sank down in the chair again. "Susan is. Barrett's her brother. They're nice and know all sorts of things about almost everything."

"Do they go to our school? I don't remember them."

"They moved here a month or so ago from Chicago," Addy said. "Susan is so stylish, and Barrett is a real scream. He's terribly witty."

Harry raised his eyebrows a bit. Terribly witty, this fellow was. Harry was certain he had never heard Addy call anyone witty before. "They sound, uh, nice," he said.

"They are," Addy replied, her voice rising higher. "And they know how to have fun. Unlike my parents."

"What is all this about your parents and clothes and hair? What are you so upset about?"

"You just don't understand, Harry." Addy jumped up once more.

"So, explain," Harry demanded as reasonably as he could. Addy was acting oddly. Generally she was predictable and steady. It was usually left to him to jump into trouble with both feet.

"My parents say it's frivolous to worry over your clothes and hair when there are so many more important problems to solve in the world." She shook her head a little and raised her eyes to the sky. "I just want to be like everyone else. I want to have fun, not be serious all the time."

"Your parents don't seem that bad to me." As soon as the words were out of Harry's mouth, he knew he had said the wrong thing. He could tell by the flash of anger he saw on his cousin's face.

"What would you know, Harry Allerton? Your parents are normal. They let you do whatever you want. You don't know what it's like to be a freak!" The words were practically hissed as Addy tried to keep her voice low. She grabbed the screen door handle, flung the door open, and stomped into the hall. With a last angry look at Harry, she ran up the stairs.

Harry caught the door and looked up the staircase. A door slammed in the distance.

"Where's Addy?" Aunt Esther's question from the doorway of the living room made Harry turn that way.

"She went upstairs," he said and pointed. His mind was totally confused. What on earth was wrong with Addy?

"I see," Aunt Esther said with a frown as her gaze shifted to the stairs. "Harry, why don't you go in the living room with your uncle Erik? There's a special broadcast coming on the radio about the Lindbergh flight. You'll want to hear it." Aunt Esther smiled and motioned him in the door and toward the living room. "I'll just check on Addy."

9

Harry hesitated as he watched his aunt climb the stairs. He heard the scratchy voice of the radio announcer coming from the living room. He shrugged and slipped into the room to sit near the big floor radio. Uncle Erik sat in his chair nearby. He lowered his newspaper for a moment to say hi. Harry wanted to hear the latest news about the Lindbergh flight. Whatever Addy thought, he knew that it was an important event.

Harry thought about how Addy had acted. The pair had been more than cousins the last few years; they had been best friends. He never remembered her talking this way before. She was sweet natured and only got angry when seriously pushed. Why had she changed so suddenly?

Harry knew that Addy's parents were serious. Mother said it was because they had been through some tough times when they were young. Their strictness had never seemed to bother Addy, until now.

The radio crackled, and an announcer began speaking in excited tones. "The world has been thrilled by news of the young aviator's daring flight across the treacherous Atlantic. In what is perhaps the boldest feat of our century, Charles Lindbergh has shown once again the courage and fortitude that is America's."

The hair on the back of Harry's neck stood up. Radio announcers often exaggerated their stories, but this time he agreed with every word. Outside the living-room window, white clouds had piled up, maybe getting ready for a late afternoon thunderstorm. What would it be like to fly through those clouds? Harry wasn't sure that he would ever know for himself. He had wanted to talk to Addy about flying, but she wasn't interested. The old Addy would have wanted to hash over everything related to the flight. The old Addy would already be writing a poem in honor of the great event.

He turned back to stare at the dials on the front of the radio. So how could he get the old Addy back? That was the question. He didn't know the answer—not yet anyhow—but he was going to find it one way or another.

"What do you think of all this, Harry?" Uncle Erik asked after the broadcaster had finished and a commercial began.

"It's so exciting," Harry said. "I wish I could have been in Paris when Lindbergh landed."

"I read that the crowd mobbed his plane. Some friends had to sneak him into an airfield building."

"Do you know if it's true that his plane's fuel tank was set in front of the cockpit, blocking his vision?" Harry asked.

"I did hear that. He wanted to keep from being crushed between the engine and fuel tank if the plane crashed." Uncle Erik walked over to the radio to switch stations.

"How did he see?"

"Good question. I'll have to ask around at the paper. See if anyone else knows." Uncle Erik sat down in his chair again. "Have you been out to Wold-Chamberlain lately? I know you and Addy used to go watch the planes take off and land."

"I have, but not with Addy." That was a good idea, too. The cousins used to ride their bikes out to the airfield together at least once a week. Harry's older brother, Larry, had first got the cousins interested in airplanes. When he was younger, he had plastered the walls with pictures of airplanes and pilots. It had seemed natural for Harry and Addy to like airplanes, too. Maybe going to the airfield again would remind Addy of all the fun they had together. It might help take her mind off her troubles and get her back to the good old Addy he liked. It was worth a try.

"Harry." Addy stood in the living-room door. "Could I talk to you for a minute?"

Harry approached his cousin warily. She looked calm, but he wasn't taking any chances. He followed her out into the hallway.

"I'm sorry. I shouldn't have blown up at you that way. It was rude of me," Addy said softly.

"That's all right. I guess I didn't do so good, either," Harry replied.

"I still shouldn't have said those things." She smiled slightly. "I'll try to do better. So is the broadcast over?"

"Yes, but I'll tell you about it if you like, and Addy, I was thinking that we should go out to the airfield this week, maybe on Wednesday. We haven't done that in ages. What do you say? It will be fun."

"I don't know." Addy's words came slowly. "I have so much to do. I don't really have time."

"Aw, come on. It's summer. What better things can you have to do?" Harry stopped because Addy's eyes were flashing with anger again. He grinned, hoping to distract her.

"You're impossible. But I'm not going to let you get me riled." Addy crossed her arms and gave Harry a stern look that soon dissolved into a smile.

"Please, say you'll go, just this once."

The phone jangled behind them. Addy jumped at the sound, then dove for the telephone on the table nearby.

"Addy? Will you go?" Harry called to her.

"Oh, all right. I'll go. But I can't stay all day." Addy grabbed the phone receiver. She raised her eyebrows at Harry. "You hear me?"

Harry nodded with a big smile. So far so good. Maybe the old Addy was just hidden a little. He'd find her one way or the other. She turned her back to him as she talked softly on the phone. The living-room clock chimed four o'clock. He'd better go home and do his chores. He told Uncle Erik good-bye and started down the hall past Addy. Her back was still turned, and he heard her laugh brightly.

"You are positively hilarious. I don't know how you think of all these things." Addy's voice was warm and relaxed.

Harry slowed. He wondered who she was talking to. He wasn't trying to eavesdrop, but he did have to pass her to get out the front door.

"Barrett, that's sweet of you to say, but not true." Addy listened a moment and then giggled. "I am not, you're just saying that."

Barrett it was. Harry frowned. He was probably telling her again that she was the bee's knees. He tried to slip quietly behind Addy, but in doing so he brushed against an umbrella stand that clattered loudly to the polished hardwood floor.

She whipped around to face him. "Harry, what are you doing here?" She covered the mouthpiece of the telephone

13

with her hand. "Eavesdropping, I suspect."

"Just trying to leave, if you don't mind." Harry gave her an indignant look but retreated out the front door and down the sidewalk. He was glad to get on his bicycle and shoot home. Let Addy talk to her new friend. Maybe it would put her in a better mood.

CHAPTER 2
Sparks Fly

Harry was surprised when Addy didn't back out of her promise to go to the airfield with him. He hadn't intended to listen to her phone conversation, and maybe she knew that. When he telephoned her the night before their scheduled ride to make sure she wanted to go, nothing was said about the eavesdropping. She mentioned again that she wanted to get home early but otherwise seemed excited to visit Wold-Chamberlain just like they used to. Now if he could just get this painting finished.

"Fred, can't you hurry? Just a little?" Harry said to his

younger brother. It was late Wednesday morning, and Fred stood on one side of the old shed in their backyard, slowly stroking a paintbrush over the rough wood. "Paint faster or we'll be here all day," Harry instructed.

Harry wiped sweat off his forehead. They had been painting all morning, and he was ready to be done. "At least let me do the high part." So far Fred had insisted on doing his part by himself, even though at seven, he was too short to paint the top section of the shed wall. Harry had already finished three sides of the building.

"Please, I've got other things to do after we get these brushes cleaned." Addy would be there any minute.

Fred frowned but nodded. He moved over so Harry could reach up above and paint the two-foot strip that was left.

"Hi there, cousins," Addy said from the back porch. "Hard at work I see."

"Almost done," Harry said. "It took longer than I expected." He jerked his head toward his little brother. "I'll be ready in just a few minutes."

"Take your time. I'll watch you two work." Addy walked over and sank down on the grass under a big oak tree a few feet away.

"Did you see what I did, Addy?" Fred asked. "I painted all of that." He pointed at the shed with his paintbrush.

"I see, and it looks wonderful. You did such a good job."

Harry dabbed the brush at the last bare spot. Now Addy was sounding like Addy. She'd always been crazy about Fred and often insisted they take him along on outings. Maybe she hadn't changed after all.

At last they were done and the brushes cleaned. Mother, who by then was busy scrubbing paint from Fred, told Harry and Addy to get something from the kitchen for lunch. They grabbed some leftover chicken and a couple apples and hopped on their bicycles. Munching as they peddled, the cousins headed for the airfield.

Addy pitched an apple core into a nearby ditch and turned to Harry. "So what are you going to do about working this summer now that Mr. Chambers has sold his store?"

"I'm not sure." Harry had worked after school and half days in the summer in Mr. Chambers's hardware store for over a year. The store's new owner had three sons of his own, so Harry wasn't needed. "My mother says that I may be out of a job, but I'm not out of work. She has a list of chores."

Addy giggled. "That's why you were painting."

"Exactly. We're about halfway down the list. School is sounding pretty good."

"Barrett works in a clothing store. He says it's boring, but the pay is good and he can get off whenever he likes." Addy reached up and pushed her hair back. "He knows practically everything there is to know about clothes."

"Really?" Harry gave his apple core a heave and shoved the empty paper bag down in his bicycle basket. He scratched at a splotch of paint that he had missed cleaning from his forearm. Doubtless the incredibly capable Barrett would have been neater. "What does his father do for a living?"

"Oh, Susan and Barrett's parents are dead. They live with their uncle."

17

"That's too bad. What happened?"

"It's a sad story. Susan told me that their father died in the war and their mother soon after in the flu epidemic." Addy pushed her hair back again. "Their uncle took them in. He's the colorful sort. Not what you would expect."

"What's their uncle do for a living?"

"Some kind of businessman is all I know," Addy replied. "I don't remember it being this far to the airfield the last time we came." She put her foot down and stopped for a moment.

"It's probably the heat," Harry said, "but we're here now." As they wheeled into the graveled area by the hangars, a silver and gray biplane took off. The plane raced down the runway until suddenly it lifted into the air. Sometimes Harry thought it was like the tricks he had seen at a magic show—so unexpected and unexplained was the way the plane lifted up.

"It's already out of sight," Addy said as she shaded her eyes and looked west. "It must be wonderful to be free to go wherever you please."

"Until the fuel runs out."

Addy didn't seem to hear him. She was still watching the sky. "Barrett and Susan fly all the time. They've been to New York and San Francisco and lots of other places. They say it gets to be old hat before long."

Harry found that hard to believe, but then he hadn't flown since that day four years ago when he was ten years old. He wasn't sure if he would ever be able to fly again, although he wanted to more than anything. He had been miserably airsick on his first airplane ride. It wasn't an

18

experience he wanted to repeat. Yet he loved airplanes; and the thought of flying, when he could get past his fears of getting sick again, excited him a great deal.

Lost in his own thoughts, Harry suddenly realized that Addy was still talking about the ever noble Barrett. Maybe it wasn't fair, but he didn't like that fellow, and he had never even met him.

The cousins parked their bikes and walked around to the front of the hangars. It was quiet. Harry didn't see any other planes ready to take off, and the sky overhead was empty of incoming traffic. In fact the only evidence of anyone else was the sound of humming that seemed to come from the engine of a nearby plane. Harry peered under the plane's gray belly and saw legs, two of them.

"Come on and meet my friend," Harry said and motioned for Addy to follow. He led the way around the plane.

"Hi there, Ernie," Harry said. The legs were attached to a body whose head was leaning deep inside the airplane's engine. The humming stopped abruptly, and a head appeared sporting a huge grin on a grease-streaked face.

"Well, if it isn't my mechanical wizard friend." Ernie pulled a rag from his back pocket and wiped his hands, although Harry doubted that the black bit of cloth would soak up much more grease.

Harry introduced Ernie to his cousin and added, "Ernie's the mechanic here at the airfield, but he used to be a barnstormer."

"I'm purely pleased to meet you, Miss Addy," said Ernie with another big grin as he swept off a filthy cap that covered a mop of brown hair. "Your cousin speaks highly of you."

Addy grinned in return. The trio talked for a few minutes before the sound of an airplane circling the field drew their attention.

They looked up as the plane made its approach and lined up with the runway. Harry recognized it as one of the mail planes that landed regularly, carrying mail for Minneapolis and outlying towns. He listened to the motor's sound and after a moment or two frowned. "Sounds a bit off, wouldn't you say, Ernie?" Harry asked.

The mechanic said nothing, but Harry saw him tilt his head slightly and frown in concentration.

"What do you hear?" Addy asked, but Harry motioned for her to listen.

In a few moments Ernie turned to Harry. "You're right. One of the cylinders isn't firing properly. Probably nothing serious—could be just a bad spark plug—but it has to be checked out."

"You're not telling me that you could tell that just from listening to the motor of that plane?" Addy asked.

"Yep, old Harry here has the ear of a mechanic, not to mention the hands," Ernie said. "It's mighty helpful to have talents that make your work easier."

Addy nodded. "I guess so. I know my friend Barrett is a real genius at picking clothes. That helps him in his job at a clothing store."

Harry rolled his eyes. "Picking clothes is a lot different from fixing airplanes."

"I guess I know that," Addy said hotly. "You make it

sound like fixing airplanes is more important."

Harry shrugged. He did think that, but maybe now wasn't the time to express his opinion.

"The good Lord made us all different for a reason," Ernie said, starting toward the mail plane as it taxied off the runway. "Now somehow I just can't see Harry being too good at selling clothes, any more than this Barrett is likely to understand engines the way Harry does." He stopped and looked Harry up and down with exaggerated care. "Seeing as how Harry is a little lacking in the fashion department."

Addy giggled. "I see what you mean."

"I resent that remark," Harry said but grinned as he looked down at himself. His shirt was partly untucked from his pants, and one shoe was untied. There was a splotch of something brown, probably oil, on the front of his shirt. It had never occurred to him to care how he looked. His mother did all the caring that got done. She was better at that. Of course, maybe that was the case with Barrett, too. If picking clothes was his talent, then that was what he should do. All Harry knew was that he was tired of hearing about the wonderful Barrett.

He helped Ernie work on the mail plane, while Addy watched. A bad spark plug had caused the cylinder to miss. In a short time they had changed it and checked the rest of the engine.

"Harry, I really need to go," Addy said. "We got off to a late start, and I have to get back."

"Why the rush? We've hardly been here an hour," Harry said after he helped Ernie push the plane out of the hangar.

"I said I needed to get back early."

"But it's way early," Harry said. The mail plane pilot had fired up the engine and waited in the cockpit while Ernie listened. Harry listened intently, too. He thought it sounded good, but he waited and watched Ernie's face. At last the mechanic grinned and gave a thumbs up sign to the pilot, who waved back. In seconds the plane rolled down the runway, gathering speed until it lifted gently into the air. The roar became a soft drone that disappeared with the plane into the clouds.

"Harry, we've got to leave," Addy said.

"We haven't even gone to the terminal building yet," Harry said. "Let's do that and then we'll go."

"No!" Addy said sharply. "Let's go now!"

Harry blinked at her tone of voice. "What's the matter anyhow? Is Barrett supposed to call?"

"That's none of your business and, furthermore, I can go without you." With that she walked over behind the hangar, grabbed her bike, and was soon peddling furiously down the road, leaving Harry to stare after her.

CHAPTER 3

Harry Meets the Expert

"Miss Addy is quite the little spitfire when she's riled," Ernie said with a chuckle.

Harry shook his head. "She never has been before. I don't know what's wrong with her." He fell into step with Ernie as they went into the hangar and back to the shop. "Somehow she's changed, and I can tell you that I don't like it much." He nodded his head for emphasis.

Ernie chuckled again. "She's got a mind of her own. That's for sure."

"Everything gets her all excited. I keep saying the

wrong thing, but I don't even know it until it's too late."
Harry jammed his hands in his pants pockets. His plan to
get Addy's mind off her troubles seemed to have backfired.

"It might be that you should listen more and talk less
where Miss Addy is concerned. It's not easy being a
young woman these days," Ernie said. "The world has
changed a lot, especially for women."

"All she ever wants to talk about is that Barrett fellow.
I'm tired of hearing how wonderful he is."

"A little jealous, are we now?"

"No, I'm not," Harry said firmly. He scuffed his feet a
time or two in the dirt. "Well, maybe a little," he admitted, "but mostly I'm not sure this Barrett and his sister are
people Addy should have for friends."

Ernie reached for a wrench lying on the dirt floor in
the hangar. "That might be, but there's not much you can
do about it if she won't even talk to you. Better be making your peace with her and go from there."

"I guess you're right," Harry said. "I'll go find her and
see if we can't get things worked out. It's a cinch that
she'll never get back to normal this way."

"Don't forget, son, that normal for you may not be the
same for her. The little lady is growing up."

Harry frowned but nodded. Surely growing up didn't
mean that Addy would be so different. No, he didn't
agree with Ernie about that, and he was still determined
to find a way to get the old Addy back. But the first step
was to find her and apologize. Then maybe they could get
back on track.

He had started for his bike when Ernie called to him,

"Hold your horses there. I want to ask you something." He pulled the black rag out and wiped his hands again. "I've been thinking on a proposition for you, but with one thing and another, I haven't got you asked yet."

"What is it?"

"How about working here at the airfield with me this summer? I need some help at least a few hours every day, and you know your way around an engine. If you can push a broom and tidy up a workbench half as well as you change a spark plug, then you're the man for me."

"Do you mean it?" Harry felt his heart jump into his throat. To get paid for working on the engines that he loved would be a dream come true. He'd work for free if it came right down to it.

"Of course, I mean it," Ernie said. "The only problem I see is that it's a long way out here for you to ride your bike every day."

"I can do it. I don't mind." Harry knew he'd ride to the far side of St. Paul and back if it meant a job at the airfield.

"Good, then," Ernie said, "I'll see you tomorrow afternoon. Now be off with you. Find Miss Addy and make your peace."

"Oh, sure. I will. I'm going." Harry's words tumbled out. He had forgotten already that he had to make things right with Addy. But now he had something exciting to tell her.

He was surprised to see Addy sitting on her front porch again. After she had been in such a hurry to get home, he hadn't been sure she'd be there. She sat in the same chair as before, but this time she was staring into the distance.

"Addy," he said quietly. She turned and smiled faintly at him. Her previous anger seemed to have vanished. Harry decided on the direct approach. Maybe that way he could manage not to say anything wrong. "I'm sorry I wasn't ready to go when you wanted to. I was thinking about airplanes and such, but I knew you wanted to leave."

"Never mind. I guess it wasn't as important as I thought that I get home so soon," Addy said and gave a sigh so big that Harry thought it must have begun at her toes.

He started to ask her what she meant but caught himself. That was the sort of question that got him in trouble. "Ernie asked me to work at the airfield this summer."

"That's terrific! Why, that's the perfect job for you." Addy perked up, and Harry saw a spark of the cousin he used to know in her eyes.

"I know," Harry said, "and I can't wait. I start tomorrow." He was just about to go on when the phone rang in the hall.

Addy bolted from her chair as if a bee had stung her and in three seconds flat was lifting the receiver from its cradle. After she said hello, her voice dropped to little more than a whisper. Harry didn't know who it was, of course, but he had a suspicion when Addy laughed softly.

He stuck his head in through the screen door. "Addy?" He wasn't sure if he should sit down and wait or what.

She turned to him, her face flushed, and covered the receiver with her hand. "Harry, I'm sorry. I'll be busy for a while. I'll talk to you tomorrow." She started to turn away

26

again, then pivoted. "It's really exciting about your job."

Harry nodded and slipped out the door. Just as he was stepping off the top porch step, he heard a louder giggle, and Addy said, "Oh, Barrett, you're so crazy."

Anger surged through him. It was the great Barrett again. That must have been why Addy was so dejected earlier. Barrett hadn't called on time. Harry slammed the front gate and grabbed his bicycle. This guy was beginning to get on his nerves.

By Saturday, Harry was over his irritation. In fact hc had talked himself into thinking the best about Barrett and Susan until there was some good reason to think otherwise. Maybe they wouldn't be so bad.

Mrs. Boyd, his Sunday school teacher way back in fourth grade, had talked about that more than once. She had said that God expected them to be kind to everyone unless there was a good reason not to, and even then she leaned toward just removing yourself from that person's presence.

So Harry decided he'd wait to meet Barrett and Susan. He wasn't sure when that would be because he was so busy with his new job.

Saturday afternoon, at his mother's insistence, Harry had taken the streetcar downtown to one of the big department stores to buy some new shoes. Trusted for the first time to shop by himself, he had wasted no time in getting a pair of shoes exactly like the old ones.

With that done, he had time to watch construction on the Foshay Tower, a big building some rich guy was building. Father said it was going to be the tallest building in the city when it was done. It was supposed to look like the Washington Monument in Washington, D.C. Right now it was shorter than his school, but dozens of workers were busy with hammers and saws. Finally Harry tore himself away. He rode the streetcar as far as his favorite radio store. There he found a tube he needed and some other parts for his radio.

Ten minutes later he raced for the streetcar, but it was just pulling away. Rather than wait for the next one, Harry decided to walk home. It was a fine day, and he was feeling cheerful and energetic. His job was going great, although it was a long ride out there and back. After only three days of back and forth, already his legs were sore.

He hadn't talked to Addy, but she had waved to him from her father's car that morning when Uncle Erik had delivered some books to Mother from Aunt Esther. Maybe things were going better for her, too.

Harry strode along a street that had mostly warehouses with an occasional small shop. In a gap in the storefronts was a garage with a sign that promised FLAT TIRES FIXED CHEAP. It was a typical small auto repair shop with motor parts spilling out of the doors, along with all sorts of tools and other junk. But leaning haphazardly against the edge of the big garage door was a motorcycle.

Harry slowed and stopped in front of the machine. The motorcycle was old. It had two flat tires, a bent fender, and was totally covered with oily dirt. A "For Sale" sign sat propped on the handlebars.

An idea formed slowly in Harry's mind as he knelt to

inspect the small motor. There was nothing obviously wrong, although he knew from experience that didn't mean it would run. All he could say for sure was that it seemed to have all the right parts. He looked at the frame carefully. In spite of the bent fender, it appeared straight. The cycle also had a second seat, an oddity that he had rarely seen before.

Harry stared at it for a few moments, thinking. He needed a faster way to get to the airfield every day. Why not a motorcycle? Of course his mother wouldn't think it was such a good idea, but he might be able to convince her. His father—well, Harry wasn't sure about him. Father was fond of saying that young people should be open to new experiences, but being a doctor also made him aware of safety. It could go either way.

"Interested in this fine machine?" a voice asked from the depths of the garage. A man stepped out into the sunshine and walked over to Harry. "Quite a bargain, too."

The man was covered from head to toe with oily dirt. It was impossible to tell how old he was. Like Ernie, he scrubbed vigorously at his hands with a rag that was itself black with dirt.

"Had a little run-in with an oil pan this morning," the man said and gave the rag a swipe across his face, which only smeared the dirt.

"What do you want for this cycle?" Harry asked.

"Now you're one to get right to the point," the man said as he placed a greasy hand on the cycle's seat. "As you can see, this is a classic machine, built to last. It's been well lubricated and kept in storage."

Harry swallowed a chuckle. The cycle was clearly

29

old, covered with dirt, and had been sitting somewhere so long that the tires had dry-rotted. To the man he only asked again, "How much?"

"I think fifteen dollars should do it."

"Too high," Harry said and backed up a step. "It's not worth half that."

"You shock me, lad," the man said and shook his head slowly. "I'll take twelve dollars and not a penny less."

Harry continued to back up. "No, I don't think so." He turned to leave.

"Ten dollars," the man barked, "and that's my final price."

"I'll think about it and let you know," Harry called and started down the sidewalk. He could hear the man muttering about young whippersnappers. Ten dollars wasn't a bad price, but that was all the money he had saved, and the motorcycle would have to have new tires and some other parts.

He walked fast, in a hurry to see if Father was back from the hospital yet. Harry knew Father would listen to his idea, even if he didn't agree.

As Harry hurried past a drugstore a few blocks from home, he saw a familiar head through the store window. Addy sat at one of the tiny tables near the soda fountain with a young man. As Harry peered through the window, a white-aproned man put two soda glasses on the table in front of them. His cousin was laughing and talking as she took the straw in her hand and sipped.

Harry hesitated as he thought. Probably this was the magnificent Barrett. Why Addy was here alone with him was a puzzle, but nonetheless, it was an opportunity to meet the new friend or, as Addy had described him, the new friend's brother. If Harry were serious about trying to like this fellow and his sister, he'd have to meet them. With Mrs. Boyd's admonitions about kindness in his mind, he nodded his head. He was going to try.

With that decision made, Harry pushed open the door to the drugstore. A big ceiling fan stirred the air, making the interior feel cooler than the hot sidewalk. Harry walked right over to Addy's table.

"Hi, Addy."

She jerked her head around. The broad smile on her face froze for just a moment before she gave a nervous giggle. "Harry, what are you doing here?"

"Just passing by and saw you through the window. Thought I'd stop and say hi." He nodded in a friendly fashion at the young man sitting by Addy. Harry suddenly realized that he was in fact a young man, not a boy. He had to be at least eighteen.

"Oh, yes, well it's good to see you," Addy said with a smile, but he could see something else in her eyes, some other reaction. Harry wasn't sure exactly what it was.

"This is Susan's brother, Barrett Kelly," Addy continued. "Of course, I guess you haven't met Susan, either. She was supposed to join us, but there's no sign of her yet. I don't know where that girl is." Addy laughed, but once again there was something in her eyes besides humor.

It might be irritation, Harry decided, or maybe confusion, or guilt.

"My sister is totally undependable when it comes to

appointments," Barrett said as he stood to shake Harry's hand. "It's a pleasure to meet you, Harry. Addy speaks often of her young cousin, the one who is wild about machines." He gave Addy a warm glance that didn't escape Harry's notice.

Addy blushed but recovered quickly and asked, "Harry, what exactly brings you here? You've been working all the time lately."

Harry lifted the paper bag that he carried. "New shoes. My mother insisted. I missed the streetcar, so I walked."

"Shopping for new footwear," Barrett said. "So many choices. Let's see what you came up with." He took the bag from Harry's outstretched hand and peeked in it.

"Just plain old shoes," Harry said and tried to pull the bag back, but Barrett had already withdrawn the box. He flipped open the box, took out the shoes, and held one up.

"Interesting," Barrett said. "Serviceable to be sure, but a bit on the unimaginative side, my boy." He held the shoe gingerly between two fingers as if it already smelled of a dirty foot rather than the fresh new leather that Harry had sniffed earlier.

"It's just a plain old shoe," Harry repeated. But even to his eyes, the shoe now looked dull and clumsy.

"Of course it is," Barrett said. "And a perfectly fine shoe at that. Not everyone wants to pay attention to their apparel, and that's just fine." He carefully put the offending shoe back into its box.

"Barrett knows ever so much about clothes," Addy said with an admiring smile at the young man, who was now brushing an invisible speck of lint from his shirtsleeve.

"Oh, does he now?" Harry murmured under his breath. To Addy he said, "Enough about shoes. Guess what? I found an old motorcycle for sale. If I could buy it and fix it up, I'd have a faster way to get to my job."

"That would be wonderful," Addy said. "Would your parents let you buy it?"

"I'm not sure, but they might, since it would be for transportation."

"What kind of cycle is it?" Barrett asked.

"I think it was a Harley-Davidson," Harry answered.

Barrett frowned. "That's not good. I'd only buy an Indian if I were you. They are the best motorcycles being manufactured today."

"I don't exactly have any choice," Harry said. "This is the cycle that's for sale. I'm not likely to find another one I can afford."

"That is a problem," Barrett said. "But I'd still think twice about buying anything but an Indian. Quality counts, you know."

Irritation pricked at Harry's resolve to like this friend of Addy's. "I agree, but I think a Harley will be just fine."

"Barrett knows about motorcycles, Harry," Addy said. "You'd better listen."

"I am listening, Addy," Harry said emphatically. "But I can't help it if the only motorcycle I can afford isn't an Indian."

"You needn't get cross about it," Addy said. "Barrett's just trying to help." She smiled sweetly at the young man, who smiled back and patted her arm.

"I'm not cross," Harry said. He was about to say more

33

when the door of the drugstore was flung open to reveal a girl with brown bobbed hair, short skirt, and a definite air of purpose.

"There you are," she said dramatically. "I'm so sorry to be late." The girl swooped over to the table where Addy and Barrett sat. Harry remained standing.

"Susan, you are a naughty girl to keep us waiting." Barrett waved lazily, but Harry noticed that he didn't stand while Susan took the other seat.

"I can see, dear brother, that you waited for me." Susan pointed at the now empty soda glasses on the table.

Barrett shrugged and grinned.

"Addy, darling, how are you?" Susan said and looked curiously at Harry, who felt he was being inspected like a chicken at the butcher's shop.

"This is my cousin Harry," Addy said.

"The young man who loves those nasty old engines," Susan said. "So dirty and noisy but necessary. If I'd had Uncle's car this afternoon, I wouldn't be so late." She turned a beaming smile on Harry, who felt a sudden desire to retreat.

"Harry may buy a motorcycle," Addy announced.

"An Indian, I should hope," Susan said firmly. "The only kind. They've been around forever."

At this Harry decided that he had been around long enough himself. "I'll be going now," he said. "Nice to meet you both. See you later, Addy."

Finally he was on the sidewalk again, headed toward home. What a pair Addy's new friends made. He had a sinking feeling that it was going to be a lot harder to like them than he had hoped.

CHAPTER 4

Keep Your Eyes on the Road

It was only the end of May, and already the church was swelteringly hot when it filled up with people for Sunday morning services. Harry and Addy sat near a window to catch any stray breeze that might drift in. Harry was tired from his busy week and glad to sit still for a while, even in the heat. When he was younger, Harry had often used the quiet of Sunday morning services to plan schemes and practical jokes, but nowadays he tried to steer his brain to listen to the sermon.

Today the minister preached about joy in the Lord. He

talked about how the Bible told them to shout for joy and make a joyful noise. Harry smiled a little to himself. Joy was something he understood and looked for, so he was glad that God approved. Addy stirred beside him. Harry wondered if his cousin was feeling enough joy lately. She hadn't said much before or after Sunday school, and she had seemed quiet even for Addy.

Harry pondered joy again. An image of the whole congregation suddenly jumping up and shouting for joy caused him to chuckle softly. As if on cue, both his mother and Addy turned to him. Addy smiled, but his mother's eyebrows were raised in a "what in the world are you laughing in church for" sort of look. Harry quickly looked down. Before he could get himself in real trouble, the minister announced the closing hymn.

The Moes and the Allertons ate Sunday dinner together at Addy's house. After a big meal, everyone retreated to the shaded front porch, trying to rest and stay cool. The adults lounged on the porch furniture, talking, while Harry and Addy took turns playing checkers with Fred on the cool boards of the porch floor. Harry's older sister Gloria had draped herself across the porch swing, where she remained, reading a book.

It was the kind of Sunday afternoon that Harry loved. It was like a hundred other afternoons spent with Addy and her family. Harry reveled in the familiar feel after the ups and downs of the past week with Addy. He felt optimistic that everything was going to work out just fine.

"I hear you've found a motorcycle, Harry," Uncle Erik said.

"An old one, but it looks fixable," Harry replied. His parents were considering his idea, although his mother's eyes had grown large when he told her about the cycle.

"I remember that you had a cycle once, Richard," Uncle Erik said.

"That I did," Father replied with a fond smile. "It was right after the war started. I was trying to save gasoline."

"I didn't know that," Harry said. His face perked up with interest.

"It was a short-lived venture, thank goodness," Mother said firmly. "That machine was broken down more than it was running. Not to mention that your father about turned my hair gray a couple of decades early when he took me for a ride."

Father grinned sheepishly. "I was a bit inexperienced, but I got better."

"What do you know about kinds of motorcycles, Father?" Harry asked. He pushed the red checkers over to Addy so she could play the next game with Fred.

"I know some. Why do you ask?"

"Well, yesterday afternoon at the drugstore, Addy's friend Barrett said that the only decent motorcycle was an Indian. He didn't think it was a good idea to buy this one since it was a Harley-Davidson." No sooner had Harry's words spilled out than Addy gave him a sharp look. Immediately his brain scrambled into action, trying to think what he had said or done to cause that look.

"I don't know a lot about motorcycle brands, but I've certainly heard of Harley-Davidson cycles. The Indian brand might have been around a little longer, but that doesn't necessarily mean anything." Father shifted in his chair. "Maybe this Barrett knows something I don't know."

"Who is Barrett, anyhow?" Uncle Erik asked. "If he's a friend of Addy's, I haven't heard of him."

"What were you doing at the drugstore yesterday afternoon, Addy?" Aunt Esther asked after a slight pause. "I thought you were working at the Red Cross office."

Harry's pleasant feelings faded. Addy flashed him a fierce look before turning to her mother. "I stopped by on my way home."

"It doesn't seem like the drugstore would be on your way home," Aunt Esther said.

Addy shrugged, and nothing more was said on the subject. The adults resumed their conversation, and in a few minutes, Addy said she was tired of playing. Fred drifted over to climb into the porch swing, and Harry carried the game board and pieces indoors.

Addy met him in the hall. "Why on earth did you mention Barrett and the drugstore? I'll be in trouble for sure."

"How was I to know that you weren't supposed to be there?" Harry said, stepping back from the anger in Addy's voice.

"Come on, Harry. You know how my parents are. Of course I was scheduled to be off doing good works." Addy grabbed his arm and pulled him toward the kitchen.

"What is the matter with you?" Harry asked in frustration. "You don't even sound like yourself."

"I said before that there is nothing the matter with me

that couldn't be cured if my parents would just leave me alone." Addy stopped in the middle of the back hallway. "If you want to help, you'll stop blabbing about my doings."

"I don't know why you're in such a dither, but you can be sure that I'll keep my mouth shut from now on." Actually Harry wanted to wash his hands of the whole business. He did the only thing he could think of. He turned on his heel and stomped back out front. Let Addy stew in her own juices and maybe throw in that irritating Barrett and Susan for flavoring.

It was against Harry's nature to stay aggravated with Addy for long, so in a few days he was able to put the whole episode in the back of his mind. Besides, he had plenty to think about aside from Addy and her problems. The verdict was in from his parents. He could buy the motorcycle if the garage owner's price of ten dollars was still good. Father said it was bound to be worth that much if all vital parts were intact. Harry would have his first pay from his job in a few days and could get the new tires then.

With crossed fingers, Harry set off with Father to purchase the motorcycle. To his great relief, the crusty garage owner was glad to take the ten dollars. According to him, it was worth much more, but he liked to see a boy take some initiative, as he called it. So Harry was the owner of a 1912 Harley-Davidson Silent Gray Fellow, or at least that was what the garage owner said with great pride. It was rough looking, but it was his.

Harry spent his days in endless motion, leaving little

time to think about anything but work, chores, repairing the cycle, and sleep. He loved working at the airfield, but he couldn't wait to get the motorcycle running so the trip wouldn't take so long.

It took almost two weeks, but finally he was ready to put the finishing touches on the cycle. Addy had gone to Cincinnati with her mother to visit some relatives, so Harry hadn't seen her for more than a week. It was Saturday, and she should be getting home that afternoon. He couldn't wait for her to see the results of his work. He thought about her as he adjusted the motorcycle's new leather belt late Saturday morning. Maybe she'd like to take a ride with him on his new vehicle. He really should do something to show that he wasn't still angry with her. In spite of Addy's ups and downs lately, Harry wanted to be friends with his cousin.

At last the cycle was ready for the road, and Harry's father took him out in the street for some lessons. It wasn't terribly different from riding a bicycle, so within an hour or so, Father pronounced Harry ready to solo. Mother had watched the lessons from the front porch but came out to the street to advise Harry to go slow and keep his eyes on the road.

As if a person would keep his eyes anywhere else when he was driving a vehicle, Harry thought. He knew enough to keep those thoughts to himself.

By late afternoon Harry made his first trip beyond his street and into the rest of the neighborhood. He grinned when three little boys who lived on the next street pointed and yelled as he rode past them. Carefully he raised one hand to wave. This was the life. The wind whistled by his ears as the motorcycle roared beneath him. The cycle wasn't going all that fast, but he felt like he was flying.

Around the park once, he decided, and then he'd head over to Addy's and see if she was home yet. He was at the far edge of the park near the fishpond when a familiar head raised up over the edge of the stone wall that bordered the pond. It was Addy.

With a careful turn, Harry steered to the side of the small lane that ran near the pond. "Hi, there," he yelled after killing the cycle motor. Addy turned with a look of surprise.

"Harry, I didn't expect to see you here," Addy said. He saw his cousin dart a glance to both sides before walking to meet him.

"I was coming to see if you were home yet after I made a trip around the park for practice." He lowered the stand and waved a hand casually at the cycle. "I got it all fixed up."

"I see that," Addy said. "It looks great." She walked slowly around the cycle. "How did you get it to look so new?"

"Mostly elbow grease and a little paint. It's still an old motorcycle, but it should get me to and from the airfield." He polished at a tiny smudge on the handlebars. "Do you want to go for a ride? It has an extra seat."

"I don't think so," Addy said quickly. "I'm really not dressed for that." She motioned to her dress. "Besides, are you ready for passengers yet? I don't care to end up in the ditch."

Harry grinned. "I just figured that we used to ride our bikes double all the time. Can't be much harder than that."

"Maybe," Addy said doubtfully. "I think I'd rather wait."

"That's fine. Why don't I walk you home? Then I'll show the cycle to Uncle Erik."

"No, that's not necessary," Addy said. "You don't want to walk the cycle all that way. I'm sure it's heavy."

"Not that bad," Harry replied. "I don't mind. Come on."

Addy stood where she was without moving. A tiny frown turned her lips down, and she glanced left and right again. "Harry, I'm not ready to go. You go on without me."

"Oh." Harry wasn't sure what to say next. It didn't make sense to him that she would be in the park alone, but maybe she wanted to think or pray. Sometimes he climbed the big tree in the backyard for just such reasons.

"If you're sure," he said at last. At her firm nod, he rolled the cycle into the lane and started it. She waved as he roared off.

The streets were quiet for a Saturday afternoon, but as he went farther, the traffic picked up. After a few blocks he decided to turn back. He had been too excited at lunchtime to eat much, and now his stomach was growling. He knew there were some molasses cookies in the pantry, and that's where he was headed. The return trip brought him past the park once more, and he glanced over to see if Addy still sat near the fishpond.

Addy was there, and so was a low-slung automobile parked on the grass. Harry saw another figure but couldn't tell who it was. With hardly a second thought, he turned his cycle in that direction. He'd better make sure that Addy was safe.

As Harry reached the fishpond, Addy was getting into the car, assisted by Barrett Kelly. Harry looked around to see if Susan was there also, but there was no sign of the sister. *Great,* Harry thought. *What's Addy up to now?* He slowed down. What should he do? Addy was sitting in the front seat, waiting for Barrett to walk around the car.

Harry went past the pair, but craned his head backward to see what was happening. At that moment his balance shifted, and before he could correct it, he found himself heading for the shallow ditch that bordered the park. In he went with a thump and a thud. The cycle went one way, he went the other, and they both ended up on their backs looking at the sky. Or at least Harry was gazing at the fading blue of the evening sky.

"Harry! Harry! Are you hurt?" Addy ran up and knelt by her cousin. Her face was white in spite of the running.

"Just my pride," Harry muttered and sat up. He rubbed his elbow, which had met up with a small rock, and inspected his stinging knee. "I'm fine."

"What were you doing? Why did you crash?" Addy helped him up.

Harry noticed Barrett sauntering up. "I could ask you the same thing," he said in a low voice. "Why were you getting in a car with him?" Harry jerked his head in Barrett's direction.

Addy's pale face flushed, and she put her mouth up close to his ear. "That's none of your business, and I'll thank you to remember that." She dropped Harry's arm like it was on fire. "You promised to keep out of this, remember?"

"I remember," Harry said. He wanted to ask more questions, but Barrett had reached the two cousins.

"Quite a tumble there," the young man said. He eyed the fallen cycle. "I've heard that the steering mechanism on a Harley is less responsive. Could be a problem for a beginner like you. Now an Indian cycle, well, it responds like a dream, or so I've heard."

Harry ignored Barrett's words, stood up, and walked over to lift the cycle upright. This afternoon had started with such promise, and now he just hoped to somehow limp home. Addy could do whatever she pleased. That was fine with him.

CHAPTER 5

Trouble with New Friends

The motorcycle ended up less damaged than Harry. It had a scratch or two, but he was stiff and sore for days. Addy stayed away; but every time he accidentally brushed his sore elbow against something hard, he thought about her and Barrett. He wasn't sure what to do next. Should he tell someone, probably his parents, about Barrett and the car, or just leave it alone? Addy had reminded him forcefully that he had promised to stay out of her business. How could he break a promise?

The following Saturday was rainy and cool, so Harry was in his room working on his radio when Addy called right before lunch.

"Harry, let's go to the movies," she said when he answered the telephone. "I'll call Violet and Nate. My mother said they're home from their trip. We haven't been to the movies together in ages."

"Sounds great." Harry didn't hesitate. The four friends used to go to the movies every Saturday afternoon, but with part-time jobs and other activities, they hadn't been there in months. Nate and Violet had been gone on a trip to New York City with their great aunt Oriel after school got out. They lived with their aunt, and she had decided that it was time to broaden their horizons. Nate had declared, politely of course, that his horizons were quite broad enough, but Aunt Oriel had dragged him off to New York City anyhow. It would be fun to hear what Nate had to say about his trip.

"What's playing?" Harry asked. He'd go see whatever Addy wanted, but maybe they could see something other than a sticky sweet love story.

"Something called *Wings* is playing at the Orpheum," Addy answered. "It stars Clara Bow."

"Is it bird wings or maybe butterfly wings?" Harry swallowed hard at the thought of a movie about something to do with butterfly wings.

"Actually I believe it's about airplane wings," Addy said with a giggle. "It's a war movie all about flyers."

"Really?" Harry said louder than he intended. "Wow!"

"Meets with your approval, I see. I'll call the others,"

46

Addy said. "Let's meet at our corner at quarter to two. See you then." With that she hung up, and Harry followed suit before racing upstairs to put away his radio parts. He might even change his shirt in honor of the occasion. On second thought, he wouldn't change. The ever-elegant clothing critic, Barrett, wasn't invited. That was cause for celebration.

Nate and Violet waited at the meeting place by the big church. The four of them had been meeting there for years. It was midway between all their houses and on the streetcar line for downtown.

"Nate. Violet," Harry said as he dashed up to the bench in front of the church. "How was the trip?"

"Fun, lots of fun," Violet said.

"Very culturally uplifting as Aunt Oriel might say," Nate answered and tilted his nose in the air as if to indicate snootiness.

Violet gave her brother a playful shove. "He loved it."

Nate shrugged and grinned. "It wasn't so bad, I guess."

"Where's Addy?" Violet asked. "We need to get going. The movie starts at two-thirty."

"She said she'd meet me here," Harry said. "But she's been acting different lately. I don't know what's wrong with her."

Before he could say anything else, they heard pounding feet on the sidewalk, coming their way. Addy rushed up and gasped, "Late. Sorry about that. Let's go."

Without further talk, the friends ran over to climb on the arriving streetcar. They quickly fell into their usual ways of talking and teasing and joking as they rode to the Orpheum stop.

They were seated at the theater in plenty of time to watch the newsreel. It was still full of pictures about Lucky Lindy, as the famous pilot was being called. Now he was bringing his plane back to the U.S. on a ship. Harry couldn't hear enough about Lindbergh, which was just as well since the newspapers and radio were still full of the latest bits of news about the flyer.

Wings was a love story, but thankfully, Harry thought, it was much more. He sat gripping the arms of the seat during the exciting flying scenes. There were several aerial dogfights between the Germans and the British in the Great War. The planes swooped and dived in ways that made the movie look unbelievably real.

Nate jabbed Harry in the ribs. "How did they film that?" His whisper barely carried over the loud organ music that filled the theater. The music ebbed and flowed in time with the action on the big screen.

"I don't know," Harry whispered back. Just then the movie hero flyer shot down a German plane, and everyone in the theater cheered. In the midst of the most exciting part, Addy got up and pushed past Harry to leave. He glanced at her in surprise but decided that she must be going to get a drink in the lobby. She hadn't returned when the curtain came down for intermission.

"Where did Addy go?" Violet asked as the lights got brighter.

"Didn't she tell you?" Harry asked.

Violet shook her head. "I thought she went to get a drink, but she left a long time ago."

"Let's look," Nate said. The trio made their way through

the crowded aisle to the lobby. Harry didn't see Addy by the water fountain or anywhere else for that matter. Violet looked for Addy in the ladies room but came out shaking her head.

"Where is she?" Harry asked, more to himself than to the others. A tingle of fear ran through him, but he beat it back. There was no reason to believe that there was anything wrong.

"Let's look upstairs," Nate suggested. "Maybe she went to the balcony."

They ran up the stairs to the wide hallway that stretched behind the balcony. Several groups of people stood talking. Harry didn't see Addy, but then he heard a familiar giggle.

Harry, Nate, and Violet turned at the same time. There she was. Harry saw her down at the very end of the hall in a small group. Together they hurried through the moviegoers.

"What happened to you?" Harry demanded as he arrived at Addy's elbow.

"What in the world are you talking about?" Addy said and laughed.

"It's your watchdog come to rescue you." One member of the group spoke up.

Harry fought the urge to groan aloud. It was Barrett, of course, and Susan and a couple other people Harry hadn't met before.

"We didn't know where you were," Harry said. He ignored Barrett's remark. "One minute you're sitting by us, and the next you're nowhere to be found."

"I'm sure Addy can take care of herself," Barrett said airily. "She's quite the modern young woman."

"I certainly can take care of myself," Addy said. "I went out for a drink and ran into Susan. She insisted that I come up and meet their friends." She hesitated briefly. "I'm sorry if you were worried. There was no reason for it. As you can see, I'm perfectly fine."

Just then the lights in the hall blinked to indicate that the movie intermission was almost over. Harry nodded toward the stairs. "Let's get back to our seats. The movie's about to start."

"Addy, stay with us," Susan said. "I've got things to tell you."

Harry saw Addy start to say something and then stop. After a pause she said, "I better go back to my seat this time. I don't want to leave Violet alone with these two rascals." She waved a hand in Harry and Nate's direction and smiled at Violet.

Susan raised her eyebrows. "Whatever you think. They're both kind of cute." She crooked a finger at Nate. "Maybe there's room up here for everyone."

Nate blushed deep red and reached up to pull his collar away from his neck.

"Thanks for the offer, but we'd better go back downstairs," Harry answered. He looked to Nate for agreement, but the young man was staring at Susan with a silly grin on his face.

"Oh, yes, we better go back to our seats," Violet agreed, taking Addy's arm. "In fact, we'd better hurry."

The movie had resumed a few moments before they

50

dropped into their places. Harry frowned into the darkness. It was quite a coincidence that Barrett and Susan were at the same movie that Addy had suggested they go see. In a few minutes he forgot his worries as he lost himself to the story of courage and daring unfolding before him on the theater screen. To be a pilot like that must be thrilling. If only he could be sure that he would fly again.

All too soon, in Harry's opinion, the movie was over, and the four friends went outside where rain drizzled steadily.

"Addy," someone called from across the street. Harry looked over and saw Barrett and Susan standing near the car that Addy had been climbing into in the park last week.

Without a word, Addy dashed across the street. Harry looked at Nate and Violet briefly, shrugged, and followed his cousin. Nate and Violet followed as well.

"Why don't we drive you home, Addy?" Barrett offered. "This weather is atrocious."

"We'll drive all of you," Susan declared and gave Nate a slow smile.

Harry saw a frown pass over Barrett's face before he turned to Harry and the others. "That's an excellent idea. It will be a bit crowded, but we'll just cozy up."

"I don't know," Harry said. "We're supposed to be riding the streetcar home." He glanced at Nate, who once again looked thunderstruck as he stared at Susan.

"Harry, what can it hurt?" Addy asked. She frowned at him. "Why should we ride the streetcar if we don't have to?"

He gave her a look that was intended to signal politely

that none of their parents or Aunt Oriel was likely to think it a good idea to ride with Barrett. Her face only grew more stubbornly set. Clearly Addy wouldn't be riding the street-car, no matter what the rest of them did.

Harry threw up his hands in defeat. "All right. Let's ride. If Nate and Violet want to, that is." He wasn't willing to watch Addy go off alone in that car if he could do something about it.

"I guess so," Violet said. Nate nodded in agreement as well and climbed into the back when Susan motioned him inside.

In the end, Harry and Violet stuffed themselves into the back seat with Susan and Nate. Addy climbed into the front with Barrett, and with a grinding of gears that made engine-loving Harry cringe, they sped down the street.

Sped was the right word, too, Harry thought a few minutes later. Barrett raced through the streets, rounding corners with a roar and an occasional squealing of tires. As much as Harry loved to go fast, he couldn't keep from flinching at each squeal. Susan talked loudly to Nate, who appeared oblivious to anything else, while Violet's eyes got larger and larger in a pale face.

Addy laughed brightly and yelled over the engine's roar to Barrett, "This car is wonderful. It's so exciting."

"How about slowing down?" Harry yelled as he clutched the back of the front seat when Barrett swerved around a parked car.

"Don't be such a stick-in-the-mud, Harry," Addy said. "That's not like you, or at least not the Harry I've always known."

Harry was flung backward and then forward when Barrett braked suddenly. Harry saw only a glimpse of the scared face of an older woman who must have been trying to cross the street when Barrett almost ran her down. Stick-in-the-mud or not, this was crazy.

"Stop, now!" Harry yelled. The response was instant as Barrett slammed on the brakes again. At least they hadn't got back up to speed yet after the close call with the woman.

As soon as the car stopped, Harry flung open the door and jumped out. "We'll walk," he stated flatly. Violet scrambled out after him, and a sheepish Nate followed suit.

"Come on, Addy." Harry opened the front car door and glared at her. He knew it was risky to challenge her, but this guy's driving was dangerous.

She glared back at him, but in a second her face crumbled, and she too climbed out. Barrett laughed but said nothing, while Susan climbed into the front seat and waved in Nate's direction. With a squealing of tires, the pair zoomed out of sight down the street.

They weren't far from Addy's house, so the foursome turned that way. All was silent for a few minutes.

"Addy," Harry began, "I'm sorry."

"Don't talk to me, Harry Allerton," she said through clenched teeth. "Don't ever talk to me again." She walked faster.

"I said I was sorry." Harry caught up with his cousin, who stomped down the sidewalk.

"I have never been so embarrassed in my whole life.

To have to get out of Barrett's car that way was just unbelievably rude."

"He was driving like a maniac," Harry said.

"His car is built for speed, and he's a good driver," Addy insisted.

"He almost ran over that old woman!"

"He was miles from hitting her."

"Addy, you're not making sense about this." Harry could barely keep up with her, and Nate and Violet were several yards back.

"You're just jealous," she said hotly. "Finally I have some friends of my own, friends who have a lot on the ball, and you don't like it. Little Addy should stay the same as always."

"Well it's certain to me that you're not the same person." They stopped abruptly because Addy's front gate had been reached. "Did you arrange to meet Barrett at the movies today? Is that why you wanted us to go, so you'd have an excuse to see him?"

"I cannot believe you'd say that." Addy grabbed the gate so hard that it was in danger of being pulled off its hinges. "I'm not listening to this one second more. Goodbye." With that, she slammed the gate and pounded up the sidewalk.

Harry stood there. Nate and Violet joined him, and they all stared at the front door where Addy had disappeared. He sighed deeply and shook his head.

"I'm in the suds now."

CHAPTER 6

Birthday Party Blues

On Monday morning Harry went to the airfield early to help Ernie with some scheduled maintenance on two of the mail planes. He was still fuming from Saturday's fight with Addy. His cousin had pointedly sat by her mother Sunday at church instead of by him. Harry wasn't surprised, but it still hurt his feelings a little. Today he was just back to being aggravated with her.

The work went fast, and by noontime Harry was sweeping out the hangar before going home. Addy had been in the back of his mind all morning. He still didn't know what action, if any, he should take. He had figured out one thing while he was replacing spark plugs and draining oil. Addy had to be protected from Barrett and his crowd. How to do that was not something he had figured out yet.

Sweeping finished, Harry was hanging up the broom when he heard a plane landing. It was a silver monoplane that he hadn't seen before. It was still hard for him to get used to the one-winged airplanes. They looked naked without the double-decker wings of the biplanes that usually populated the airfield. Ernie said the monoplanes would eventually take over because they were better suited to flight. Harry wasn't sure he clearly understood why, but he was learning.

Ernie came out of the terminal to eye the aircraft before joining Harry. "It looks like a Wright-Bellanca. It has the same kind of engine as Lindbergh's plane and a similar body."

"How can you tell about the engine just by looking?" Harry asked.

Ernie grinned. "I cheated. The terminal manager was talking about some businessman who had ordered a new plane that was supposed to be flown in today."

"He knew what kind it was," Harry stated.

Ernie nodded. "She's a beauty, too."

The pilot climbed out of the plane, followed by two other men. One of the passengers was a short, rather portly middle-aged man, and the other was a young man dressed in the latest style. Harry strained his eyes toward the group and groaned. The young man was Barrett. How was it possible for that fellow to turn up so often?

The pilot and the older man crossed directly to Ernie and began talking about hangar space and schedules, while Barrett lagged behind.

Harry finally raised his hand in a small wave and said, "Hi, Barrett. I haven't seen you out here before."

"If it isn't Addy's big brave rescuer," Barrett said. "Jerry, isn't it?"

"Harry."

"Oh yes, Harry it is," the older boy said and adjusted his hat while managing to look bored.

"Is that your uncle?"

"Yes, and that's his new airplane," Barrett said and sniffed. "He uses it for business."

"What kind of business? I mean what kind of work does your uncle do?"

"If that were any of your affair," Barrett said lightly, "I'd tell you."

Harry backed up a step. "Sorry," he said and shrugged. This fellow was not one of those people you liked better after you got to know them a little.

"Such a joker this boy is," the portly man said, turning his attention to the boys. Evidently he had overheard their conversation. He had a big smile on his round face, and a fat cigar jutted out from his mouth.

"Now, son. I own a few drugstores and two restaurants and two or three other stores. I lose count," he said with a laugh that forced him to yank his cigar out of his mouth to keep from losing it. "The life of commerce is the life for me."

Harry couldn't resist smiling back at this jovial man who had what Harry thought was a Chicago accent. His black and white striped suit looked expensive, and he wore a bright yellow and black necktie. His manner of dressing was flashier by far than Barrett's.

"Guess you know my nephew here?"

"Yes," Harry said. "We've met a time or two." He refrained from adding that it was a time or two too many.

"This is Harry," Barrett finally spoke up. "He's Addy's cousin."

"Ah, the lovely Addy." The man popped his cigar out again and reached for Harry's hand. "Nice to meet you, Harry."

"Nice to meet you, too, sir." He did seem nice but much different from his nephew.

"Call me Uncle Marty," the man said with another burst of loud laughter. "Everyone calls me Uncle Marty."

Harry thought he saw a glimpse of discomfort on Barrett's face when his uncle laughed again and slapped Harry on the back. He couldn't be sure, because Barrett's smooth mask of coolness slid back on so quickly.

"Say, I have a humdinger of an idea," Uncle Marty said. "We're having a birthday party for Susan next Saturday. Why don't you come and bring some friends if you like? Barrett here and Susan don't know too many young people yet in Minneapolis. A party's no fun if it's just old folks." He chomped down on his cigar and nodded at his own inspiration.

Barrett allowed himself a frown. "I'm sure Harry has better things to do than come to a birthday party. He works here, you know, as a grease monkey or something like that."

"Is that right?" Uncle Marty said. "I like a boy with ambition. But now, I won't take no for an answer. Surely your employer doesn't make you work on Saturday evening? I'll just have a word with him. All work and no play makes Jack a dull boy, you know. Hey, hey. Can't have you dull."

"No, I don't have to work, but I don't know. . ." Harry's voice trailed off. What a pickle. About the last thing he wanted to do was go to a party with Barrett, and by the look on the other boy's face, the feeling was shared.

"I won't hear another word," Uncle Marty said. "Besides, sweet Miss Addy is already coming. I'm sure she'll be glad to have her cousin and some other friends there, too."

Addy was going to the party. Great. He probably couldn't talk her out of it, but he wasn't willing to let her go off with Barrett, either. Why was life so complicated lately? He would have to go to the party whether he wanted to or not just to keep an eye on Addy.

"All right," Harry said. "I'll come."

"That's more like it," Uncle Marty said and slapped Harry on the back again. "Bring your friends. It will be a real blowout of a party."

Uncle Marty walked on toward the terminal, and Barrett followed. He didn't say anything, but the look he gave Harry could have curdled milk. After he passed, Harry allowed himself a small grin. He might not want to go to the party, but it was obvious that Barrett wanted it even less. Harry's grin faded as he thought of the trouble that was likely to erupt when Addy found out he'd been invited to the party, too.

Addy wasn't as irritated as Harry had expected. He suspected that she hadn't figured out yet how to get her parents to let her go to the party. Having Harry along and maybe Nate and Violet, too, would definitely help her case. Harry thought about backing out when his mother told him that he'd have to dress up for the event. It was bad enough to have to spend an evening with Barrett, but to have to dress up was almost too much to expect of a person. In the end he knew he had no choice. Someone had to watch out for Addy.

Harry persuaded Nate and Violet to go along to the party. It wasn't hard to convince Nate, but Violet was adamant at first that she wasn't about to spend her Saturday evening with that bunch. Finally she agreed to do it since Harry thought it was so important.

Father drove the four friends to Uncle Marty's house several miles away. Uncle Marty's housekeeper had called earlier to say that the chauffeur would pick them up, but Mother had said that no child of hers was going off in a car with a chauffeur to visit people she and Father had never met. It was decided that the chauffeur could bring them home when the party ended.

Aunt Esther and Uncle Erik had to go to a dinner honoring a friend of theirs, so that cut down on the number of helpful hints about party behavior. Harry was thankful for that, since it was bad enough that he had to put on his Sunday suit with a tie.

Uncle Marty's house, which he shared with Barrett and Susan, was large and impressive. A circle drive brought the car right up in front of several tall white pillars. When they stopped, a white-coated young man jumped to open the car doors. With a wave to Father, Harry and the others climbed out and followed the servant through the huge wooden doors that stood open.

Once inside, a pink-cheeked girl in a black maid's uniform led them into a room so big that Harry could hardly remember his manners long enough to keep from throwing back his head to gaze at the ceiling. At the far end of the room was a long table of food. Several small tables were scattered here and there across the shiny tile floor. And everywhere there were vases and baskets and even buckets of fresh roses. The sweet smell drifted through the room like a breeze.

"Addy!" a voice squealed. Susan swept into the room from a doorway that led to an outdoor terrace. Harry saw several people standing outside, but the big room itself was empty.

"Happy birthday, Susan," Addy squealed in return. "These roses are wonderful."

"Aren't they? I love roses, and Uncle Marty went crazy." Susan swept a long white scarf up closer around her neck. Harry couldn't help wondering how she kept from choking herself.

"Are we early?" Harry asked. "We seem to be the only ones here so far."

"Oh, no," Susan said with another flip of her scarf. "It's just fashionable to be late. A couple of Uncle Marty's friends are out on the terrace, but other people will be here soon."

A sudden surge of music made Harry look at the other end of the room. Nearly hidden behind some large potted palms was a five-piece orchestra that played a lively tune.

"Wow!" Violet said to Harry. She sounded as impressed as he was. "This puts my last birthday party in the shade. Games in the parlor with punch and cake seems kind of dull in comparison with this." She waved her hand at the opulence that surrounded them.

"Let's go get some punch for everyone," Susan suggested. She gave Nate a pouty smile and, arm in arm with Addy, led the way toward the food table.

"See there," Harry said in Violet's ear. "We are having punch after all. Just like your party." He grinned as Violet rolled her eyes.

Punch in hand, the group sat down at a nearby table. In a few minutes Susan ran to meet two noisy groups of new arrivals that came through the door from the hall. Uncle Marty also appeared to greet these guests, who were closer to his age than Susan's. Harry wondered where Barrett was. He supposed that it was unlikely that the annoying young man would miss his sister's party. That thought had barely passed through his mind when there was a stir at the terrace door.

Barrett stood poised as if making a grand entrance. Harry stared harder.

"What in the world is he wearing?" Violet hissed in Harry's ear.

"I'm not sure," Harry answered slowly, still looking at the figure now sweeping somewhat grandly into the room. "It looks like extremely baggy pants."

Barrett's trousers sported extra wide legs that practically flapped in the wind, if there had been a wind, that is.

"Doesn't he look stunning?" Addy's voice pierced

Harry's thoughts. He looked over and saw that his cousin watched Barrett's every move with an adoring gaze.

"Stunning is right," he said. "They look awful. Who would want to wear something like that?"

"Harry, you wouldn't know fashion if it stepped on you," Addy said and gave him a disgusted look. "Those are 'Oxford bags,' and for your information they have been quite the rage in England."

"Send him over there, then," Harry muttered.

"You just watch it," Addy said fiercely, her face poked up next to his. "Don't you do anything to ruin this party."

"Good grief, Addy, why would you think that? "

She ignored his question. "Just don't do anything." With that, she rose from the table and walked toward the terrace door where baggy-pants Barrett was still striking a pose.

In a minute Susan reappeared to drag Nate off to meet a friend, leaving Harry and Violet alone at the table, sipping punch and watching the room fill up with guests.

"There don't seem to be many young people here," Violet said after awhile. "Most everyone is older. I've never been to a birthday party like this."

Harry nodded. "Me either." Some of the guests began to dance in the area in front of the orchestra. The musicians played the latest tunes and some that Harry didn't recognize.

"They're doing the fox trot," Violet said of the dancers.

So far, Harry had to admit this party had been pretty tame. Uncle Marty had come over to welcome them in his booming voice. How the man managed to talk with a cigar hanging out the side of his mouth, Harry didn't know. Susan, with Nate following, breezed back in to cut a huge birthday cake while everyone cheered. Barrett and Addy sat talking with several other guests at a table on the other side of the room.

Harry allowed himself a sigh of relief as he and Violet took their cake and other food back to a table. Maybe, just maybe, he had been too suspicious about this party. The food was delicious, the music lively, and except for his tie cutting into his neck, Harry was enjoying himself.

A commotion by the hallway door attracted their attention. A group of latecomers streamed in, laughing and talking loudly. An occasional shriek of laughter rose above the din.

"Look at those women," Violet said in a low voice. "They're flappers."

Harry's eyes opened wider. The women wore fringed skirts that ended above their knees. The tops of rolled-down stockings showed just below the fringe. Every one of the young women had extremely short bobbed hair and sported tiny, close-fitting hats. Their eyes looked unnaturally dark, and their lips were blood red.

The biggest surprise to Harry was the cigarettes that hung from their hands by way of long, sticklike holders. As Harry watched, a woman took a puff on the cigarette, blew smoke in the face of one of the men who stood nearby, and laughed loudly. Amazingly enough to Harry, the men seemed to find this behavior quite entertaining.

"Harry!" Violet's voice interrupted his study of the rowdy scene unfolding across the room. "Do you think this bunch is friends with Addy?"

Harry watched the new guests for a moment. Now they had split up, with some going to the food table and others to the terrace and a couple talking to the orchestra leader. "Doesn't seem likely, but who knows in this family."

Harry was feeling uncomfortable. He knew his parents would not approve of him being at a party with adults behaving in such a rowdy way, but he didn't want to get Addy angry at him again. She'd already warned him not to ruin the party for her.

The party grew noisier and more unruly. The newcomers were all just plain loud, whether they were eating or talking or merely walking across the room. Addy and Barrett talked to one of the couples who stood near the terrace door.

A moment later the orchestra launched into a rousing jazzy number, and as if a switch had been thrown, the flappers and their gentleman friends swarmed onto the dance floor near the orchestra. They danced in frenzy with arms and legs flying. Harry could only stare in amazement.

"It's the Charleston," Violet announced. "I saw it in New York."

"Looks a bit, uh, active to me," Harry said. "It's a long ways from the fox trot." His sister had attempted to teach him the fox trot a time or two, but she hadn't mentioned a dance like this.

"Look over there," Violet said. "At that man in the gray suit dancing with the redheaded woman. I think he has a flask in his back pocket."

"You mean a whiskey flask?" Harry craned his neck

to look for the man, who had disappeared among the energetic dancers.

"That's what I mean. It's probably full of bootlegged whiskey."

Harry frowned at his friend. He knew all about bootlegging. Nowadays everyone did. Since it was illegal to possess or sell alcohol other than for medical purposes, some people went to a great amount of trouble to get any kind of alcohol.

"We should get out of this place," Harry said. "The flask may not mean anything, but my mother would skin me if she knew that I stuck around after I saw it. I'd be in enough trouble already if she found out what's been going on."

Violet nodded. "Ditto for Aunt Oriel."

"There's Nate over there by the food, but where's Addy?" Harry asked.

"I'm not sure, but let's get Nate first."

It took awhile to detach Nate from several admiring young women who seemed to find him "so witty," as they kept telling him. By then the party was noisier than ever. The dance floor was crowded, and everywhere people stood drinking punch and laughing loudly. As he looked around the room for Addy, Harry wondered what on earth made everyone so loud. He loved to laugh and have a good time, but even he was getting a headache from the noise.

"Let's get some punch," Nate said, "and then we'll find Addy. I'm so thirsty."

"From talking so much to the lovely ladies, no doubt," Violet said to her brother as she raised her eyebrows at him.

Nate just grinned and picked up a cup of punch.

Harry looked around again for Addy as he took a sip of punch. He choked and coughed as the pink liquid hit his tongue. What in the world? He looked into the cup, but the punch looked the same. It just tasted like someone had messed up the punch recipe. It was bitter instead of sweet like it had been before.

Violet coughed so much that Nate pounded her on the back.

"What's the matter with this stuff?" Harry asked and took another tiny sip. It was bitter enough to make a person pucker up. Then it came to him. The punch had been spiked with alcohol, maybe from that same flask he and Violet had seen earlier.

"Spiked, isn't it?" Nate asked quietly.

Harry just nodded. "Let's find Addy. We've got to get out of here."

It didn't take long to find their friend. She was on the terrace with Barrett and several others. They all had cups of punch in their hands. Face flushed bright pink, Addy stood near Barrett, laughing and gesturing as she talked. Harry tried to wave to her, to get her to come to him, but if she saw him, she chose not to respond. Harry had a sinking feeling as he walked up to his cousin.

"Addy," he whispered urgently in her ear, "we need to leave now."

"Leave!" she said loudly. "It's not time to leave yet."

"Addy," he repeated firmly, "the punch is spiked. It has alcohol in it."

She seemed not to hear him. "I don't want to leave. I'm having a wonderful time." Her pink face grew rebellious.

"You're always telling me what to do. I can tell myself what to do." She promptly laughed at her own remark and swayed slightly before Harry grabbed her.

Harry gave Nate a look, and the two moved to either side of Addy.

"Come on, Addy, let's go," Harry said quietly. "Don't make a scene."

She seemed confused. "Barrett, where did you go?" She looked around the group.

"If it isn't the rescuer," Barrett said from behind them. He had a slack smile on his face, and his eyes were red. Harry made a quick judgment that from the looks of him, the other young man wouldn't be giving them any trouble.

Harry and Nate urged Addy forward. Violet extended her hand to the girl, and Addy took it. Barrett turned away to make some remark to the rest of the young people, who all laughed uproariously. Addy made no further protest and walked slowly toward the front hallway. Nate found the chauffeur, and in a few minutes they were on their way home.

Addy collapsed against the soft cushions of the seat and in seconds fell into a sound sleep.

"She's blotto," Nate announced.

"Don't say that ugly word," Violet commanded. "They gave her that spiked punch. She didn't know." After a slight pause, Violet continued, "I hope."

"The problem is," Harry said, "what do we do with her now? How can we take her home like this?" He could see that the others didn't have an answer any more than he did. He stared at his sleeping cousin. He hadn't done a very good job of protecting her, that's for sure.

CHAPTER 7

Suspicious Characters

"No car in the garage yet," Nate reported. If the chauffeur wondered why they asked him to stop down the street from Addy's house while Nate ran up in the dark to check the garage, he didn't say anything.

Addy's parents weren't home yet from their dinner. That was a stroke of luck. Harry looked over at his sleeping cousin and then at Nate and Violet. He didn't know what to do. He knew that he wouldn't lie to her parents, but since they weren't home yet, maybe there was some way to bypass that scene for tonight at least.

"Can we leave her alone?" Harry asked the others. "We could get her inside, but I don't know about leaving her alone."

Violet shook her head. "No, we'd better not do that. I'll stay the night. I think we should tell her parents what happened, but for now, we can just say that I decided to spend the night."

"Thanks a million, Violet," Harry said, relief flooding through him. "I promised her I wouldn't interfere anymore, so I'd really like to leave her parents out of this for the time being."

"I'm not sure that was such a good promise," Violet said as they attempted to rouse the sleeping Addy. "Unless this girl comes to her senses, she's headed for problems with Barrett and that bunch."

Addy missed church on Sunday morning because she was sick with some mysterious stomach ailment, according to Aunt Esther. Harry's aunt declared that it was probably from all the rich food at the birthday party the night before.

Harry sank down in the church pew and prayed. All sorts of things ran through his mind, but he kept remembering that the Bible said to be your brother's keeper. How exactly did a person do that the best way?

He was overwhelmingly relieved when Addy showed up at his house late Sunday afternoon. She looked white as a bleached sheet and was very sorry for what had happened. They sat quietly in the shade on the front porch.

"I knew the punch tasted funny, but I didn't know it had liquor in it. You've got to believe me, Harry." She put her hand up to rub her forehead.

"I believe you."

"I don't think Barrett knew, either."

Harry frowned. He wasn't so sure about that, but now probably wasn't the time to say so.

"Susan called this afternoon. She said Uncle Marty found out about the punch right after we left. He was angry and had it dumped. She didn't know why we left early, so I told her I was sick."

Addy put her hand on Harry's arm. "I'm sorry about what happened. Please don't tell my parents." Dark circles under her eyes made Addy's pale face appear older. She looked sick all right.

"I won't tell, but, Addy, this bunch is bad news," Harry said. "Please stay away from them."

"Harry, I don't blame you for being upset about this, but it wasn't Barrett's fault. He didn't have anything to do with the spiked punch."

"How do you know that?"

"I just know, that's all," Addy said. She straightened up, and Harry saw that her face wasn't pale anymore. It was flushed with anger. "You always think the worst of Barrett. He's not like that."

Harry didn't say anything. What could he say? Maybe he was wrong about Barrett, but he knew he wasn't wrong about those people at the party. "All right, Addy,

71

but be careful. Those people were scary last night."

Addy sighed her head-to-toe sigh and slumped in the chair. "I will be careful. You can be sure I won't be drinking any more foul-tasting punch." She gave Harry a tiny grin.

Harry smiled back, but he couldn't shake the feeling that his cousin still didn't understand. The relief he had felt at her apology began to slide back into worry. He had promised once again not to tell her parents, but she hadn't said she would stay away from Susan and Barrett. Maybe it was enough for her to promise to be careful, but it didn't feel like enough.

He watched her as she started down the sidewalk for home, walking slowly as if each step she took jarred her head. Her head must be pounding from the aftereffects of the spiked punch. He wanted more than anything to keep her safe, but she was making that hard to accomplish.

The next couple weeks were quiet. As far as Harry could tell, Addy kept close to home. He wondered about Susan and Barrett until Violet told him that the pair had gone to Chicago to visit friends. It seemed like a lucky break. When he saw his cousin, she still looked pale, but she asked about his job and the motorcycle.

Harry's job was going great. He loved working with Ernie and the airplanes. Day by day he learned about lift and drag and thrust and how those forces made airplanes go up or come down. Ernie had a way of teaching that didn't sound like school at all. Harry had always loved fixing things like radios and engines, but this was different.

It was hard to look at a bird the same way after Ernie explained that the way air flowed over their wings lifted them in flight.

It wasn't just the power of the engine in an airplane that caused it to soar off the ground, according to Ernie. Powerful natural forces, including gravity, were also at work. When Harry had complained that it all sounded so complicated, Ernie had just laughed and said, "Well, it is and it isn't. It's all a part of God's natural world. You don't see any birds struggling to figure out lift and drag, yet they use the same forces."

Harry had to laugh, too. The image of a bird frowning with perplexity because it was trying to figure out lift flashed through his mind. "I guess they don't at that."

"God's world fits together just like a well-maintained engine. No surprises," Ernie said. "Now let's get this engine here to fit back together." He took another wrench from the workbench and put his head inside the airplane they were working on.

A few minutes later Harry looked up as gravel sprayed on the parking lot beside the hangars. Someone was in a big hurry. Car doors slammed, and the rumble of deep voices reached Harry, but the sounds faded as the people evidently went into the nearby terminal.

Harry had just dumped some dirty oil in a can near the big front door of the hangar when a familiar figure walked up.

"Hi there, Harry."

It was Uncle Marty. Today he wore a suit made of some kind of shiny greenish material with a red and white polka-dotted tie. He looked a little like a short, plump Christmas tree except for the cigar clamped firmly in the side of his mouth.

"Hi, sir," Harry said. He wished he could remember, if he had ever known, Uncle Marty's last name. As friendly as this man was, Harry still had a hard time calling him Uncle Marty.

"So how's life treating you?" Uncle Marty asked around his cigar, giving Harry the usual slap on the back.

"Just fine, sir."

"Fine party awhile back. Glad you could come."

"Thanks for inviting us," Harry said. "The food was terrific." Years of training by his determined mother kept Harry from adding any remarks about the spiked punch.

Uncle Marty laughed loudly and went over to Ernie, who still had his head inside the airplane. A scuffing noise made Harry look back at the front of the hangar. Three men stood there. They were dressed much like Uncle Marty, except they all wore soft felt hats pulled forward to shade their eyes. There was something else different about them that Harry couldn't quite name, but a tiny shiver went up his back in spite of the hot July day. They didn't smile, and they certainly didn't laugh like Uncle Marty.

"What do you think about leasing a plane, Ernie?" Uncle Marty said. Harry looked back at his boss again. "My business associates and I would only need to lease a plane for a few weeks," Uncle Marty said. "The people in Chicago promised that it wouldn't take any longer than three weeks to make the required changes to my new plane. My pilot is taking it down tomorrow." He switched his cigar to the other side of his mouth and nodded his head vigorously. "Yes, sir, Harry, my friend. I'm fancying up my plane. You won't recognize the inside when you see it next."

The three men had walked up, and in a few minutes, Ernie led the whole group over to the terminal building to talk to the manager. Harry grabbed his broom and started sweeping near the front. Maybe he could get another look at them when they left. It wasn't long before they came out, loaded into the expensive-looking car, and drove away with another spray of gravel.

Ernie came back to stand by Harry as they both watched the car speed down the dusty road at the edge of the airfield. Ernie shook his head. "That's a rum bunch."

"What do you mean?"

"I wouldn't want to get caught in a dark alley with Marty's business associates."

"Are they crooks?" Harry asked.

"I can't say. Wouldn't be fair to judge on appearances, but I plan to keep out of their way, and you should do the same."

Harry nodded. That was no problem for him. He only hoped that Addy could be persuaded to do the same.

The very next day, Harry worked later than usual at the airfield. Two mail planes were in for repairs and needed to get back in the air as soon as possible, so Harry had stayed late to help Ernie. It was twilight when Harry jumped on his motorcycle and started home. At least he could try out the headlight on the cycle for the first time. His parents hadn't been crazy about him driving at night yet.

He was about halfway home when there was a pop and a flapping and the cycle began to weave all over the road. It was all Harry could do to stop without being tossed in the ditch like before. He peered at his rear tire. It was flat. It didn't seem like a nearly new tire should just pop. Repair shops weren't likely to be open so late, so now he was going to have to walk the cycle the rest of the way home.

Off he trudged. As he got farther into the city, there were people around, coming and going to their evening entertainment or work. But there was no sign of an open repair shop. The cycle was heavy when it was a dead weight, so he walked slower and slower. He heard a church tower chime eight o'clock in the distance, which brought him to a total stop.

His mother would be worried. He looked around the streets. He'd better find a phone somewhere and call her, just to let her know that he was on his way. Maybe his father was home from the hospital and would offer to come pick up Harry and the cycle in the auto, although the chances of the cycle fitting in the car seemed slim.

At last he found a phone in a small shop tucked among some other businesses that were all closed for the evening. Mother was glad to hear from him and sorry to report that Father wasn't home yet. He thanked the shop owner and pulled the cycle away from the wall where it was leaning. He'd just have to take it slow.

At the end of the block was a hall of some sort. People stood around talking or hurried inside the big double doors of the huge building. As Harry passed, music suddenly poured out the open windows. The people standing around immediately filed inside. The music sounded like it came from a band or orchestra. Loud and lively, it was a great deal like the music at Susan's birthday party.

Curious, Harry pushed the cycle into a tiny alley that ran along the building's side. He leaned the cycle against the building and peeked into the nearest window. The hall was crowded with young people dancing to the music of a band, whose members were much older than the dancers. The dancing couples had numbered pieces of paper fastened to the backs of their shirts and dresses.

Suddenly Harry realized what he had stumbled onto. It was a dance contest, a marathon where the dancers tried to see who could dance the longest. He had heard about dance marathons. His father said that sometimes people died of heart failure from dancing so many hours with only a short break every so often. Some contests went on for days before an exhausted couple claimed the grand prize.

The hall was brightly lit and decorated with streamers and paper flowers. It looked like fun, but Harry had seen a picture once in the newspaper of the end of a marathon dance contest. The couples looked ill and not happy at all. His mother said it was all just plain crazy.

Crazy or not, dozens of couples crowded into the hall, dancing and laughing over the loud music. Harry gave the scene a last look before leaving. Standing here wasn't going to get the motorcycle home any quicker. Just as he turned, a curly brown-haired girl on the dance floor caught his attention. She disappeared into the crowd, and he had half turned again when she bobbed back into view. Addy!

She looked little out there and younger than fourteen. Her long hair amongst the sea of bobbed hair set her apart, too. Of course Barrett was dancing with her, and Harry saw Susan nearby with a young man he recognized from the birthday party.

Harry didn't stop to think. In a flash he was inside the hall and making his way through the dancers. He grabbed Addy's arm, more roughly than he had intended. "Addy!"

Addy's first shocked look quickly turned to anger. "What are you doing here, Harry? Are you following me?"

"No, I am not following you," Harry said disgustedly, "but maybe I should be. My motorcycle got a flat tire on the way home from the airfield. I stopped to see what the commotion was, and there you were."

So far Barrett had stood back, dancing slowly while he watched the two cousins. Harry stuck his mouth up by Addy's ear so he didn't have to yell over the music. "What are you doing here? Your parents would kill you if they knew."

"Don't be so dramatic," Addy ordered and attempted to resume dancing. "It's just a contest for fun and prizes." She leaned close to Harry and said, "There's no alcohol permitted. It's perfectly safe. Look at all the adults everywhere."

Harry looked around the room. Several older people were milling around or sitting on chairs at the edge of the dance floor. He even saw a woman dressed in a white nurse's uniform.

Barrett finally spoke up, "Leave the lady alone. She doesn't need rescuing this time, either."

"Stay out of this," Harry snapped. "Addy, please. This

78

will last all night and longer. Just walk home with me."

"Harry, I know you mean well," Addy said, her arms crossed defiantly, "but I'm fine, and I'm not leaving now. So you might as well just go on home."

Not knowing any other way to convince Addy to leave, short of making a big fuss, Harry took his cousin's advice and went home. It was a long walk as he thought about Addy. First he'd worry, and then he'd be angry, and then he'd worry again. So it went all the way home as he pushed the heavy cycle.

The burden of figuring out how to help Addy felt a lot heavier than the motorcycle ever could. He had thought that she was coming around since the spiked punch episode at the birthday party, but now he felt like she was back where she started. She wanted to have fun with friends, and so far Harry had failed miserably at convincing her that these friends didn't like the right kind of fun. Miserable was how he felt as he pushed the cycle into the shed at last.

CHAPTER 8
The Secret

Harry tumbled out of bed the next morning, determined to tell his parents what he had seen the night before. After crawling into bed, he'd stared at the ceiling of his room for an hour, unable to sleep in spite of being worn out. At last he had decided that telling his parents was the right thing to do. Addy would be angry, and she might even hate him, but he couldn't handle keeping quiet any longer. Too much was at risk.

Trouble was, his parents weren't home when he went downstairs. His mother had gone to help Cousin Margaret with her newborn twin girls for a few days, and Father had to go to Cincinnati unexpectedly for a meeting. Larry was off working at his summer job, so that left Harry, Fred, and Gloria to take care of themselves for a few days. Of course Frannie, their house help, as she called herself, was there. Gloria declared herself in charge, but Harry knew that Frannie had the power.

Harry didn't know what to do since his parents were gone. In the night, when he couldn't go to sleep, he had prayed and thought God wanted him to talk to his parents about Addy. Now his parents weren't here to talk to. What was God up to anyhow? Understanding what God wanted a person to do was really hard sometimes.

He had just finished his breakfast when the telephone rang. Gloria hurried to answer. It was Aunt Esther saying that Addy wanted Fred to come over and spend the day to help make taking care of the younger Allertons a little easier on Gloria. Harry questioned Gloria after she hung up the phone. "Are you sure Addy was there?"

"I repeat, dear brother, it was Addy's idea," Gloria said. "I think she'd have to be home. She likes to play with Fred, although why she does I find totally mystifying." She grimaced as their younger brother hurtled through the kitchen on his way to the front stairs.

Addy was home. Harry wondered what had happened at the dance marathon, but it didn't really matter as long as she was safe. Now he had some time to get after her again to stay away from Barrett and Susan and that crowd. He wasn't sure if she could be convinced, but he would try.

A few days later the front page of Uncle Erik's newspaper

was full of some exciting news that pushed Harry's worries about his cousin to the far reaches of his mind. Charles Lindbergh was coming to Minneapolis!

The famous pilot was touring the United States, and Minneapolis was on his list of cities. Harry could hardly believe his eyes when he read the headline: "Famous Aviator to Land at Wold-Chamberlain Field."

By the time Harry got to the airfield that day to work, the place was bustling with city officials, airfield workers, and, it appeared, anyone else remotely connected to Wold-Chamberlain Field. Ernie was hard at work servicing a mail plane, but he looked a bit grumpy.

"Ernie!" Harry yelled from the front door of the hangar. "Can you believe it? Lindbergh coming to our field!"

Ernie gave Harry a disgusted look before breaking into his usual smile. "If I didn't believe it before, I do now. This place is swarming with people asking questions and telling me I should do this or that. I've got work to do, and so do you. Hand me that box-end wrench over there, please."

Harry put his lunch bag on the shelf and hurried to find the right wrench. "You've got to admit it's pretty exciting in spite of all this ruckus." He handed Ernie the wrench and reached for the dirty apron he usually wore when he worked.

"You're right," Ernie admitted. "It will certainly liven up our summer. I guess I'll just have to get used to all this." He waved his hand behind him at the people who milled around in front of the hangars and the terminal building. "I heard someone say that this place needed a little sprucing up. A little paint here and there couldn't hurt. We'll just have to look at the bright side."

Harry grinned at his boss. As far as he was concerned, there was only a bright side. The chance to see Charles Lindbergh was worth any amount of trouble.

He reminded himself of that many times over the next few days. The terminal manager asked him to work some extra hours painting and pulling weeds and doing general fix-up chores. That was fine, except there seemed to be a different person in charge of the preparations each day. Ernie just laughed at him when Harry complained that one day the mayor wanted him to pull weeds behind the hangars and, before he could finish, the mayor's wife told him to start painting some benches that she had found in storage. The couple had argued while Harry stood waiting.

Even with all the trouble, Harry's excitement grew daily. Addy had come down with a summer cold that kept her home for over a week. He wouldn't have admitted it to anyone, but Harry was a little glad that she was sick since it was just a nasty cold. It kept her home and safe. He was so busy that he wasn't sure he could keep up with looking out for her right now.

One day in early August, Harry put the finishing touches on a sign he had given a fresh coat of paint. The airfield buildings all sported new paint, and every weed that dared to poke its head above ground had been pulled. Closer to the big day, Harry would help put up flags and banners. He was tired from all the long hours of extra work, but it was worth it.

Paint can and brush in hand, Harry gave the sign one

last admiring look and started for the side of the hangar where he cleaned his brushes every day. A car roared down the lane and screeched to a halt in the parking lot not far from Harry.

It was a familiar auto with some equally familiar faces emerging from the doors that flew open. Addy and Susan jumped out of the back seat while Barrett unfolded his elegantly dressed figure from the front. Uncle Marty hopped out of the driver's seat, adjusted his cigar, and went toward the terminal building. A long black car pulled up behind Uncle Marty's, and the same three men climbed out who had been at the airfield before the birthday party. They still weren't smiling.

None of the visitors saw Harry because he quickly knelt over a pot of turpentine that he used to clean his paintbrushes. It was a good chance to look them over, which he did. Addy laughed as she talked to Susan and then to Barrett, who came around to her side of the car. Her face was bright with excitement.

Why did it have to be those friends who made her happy? Harry felt a twinge of guilt. His whole purpose lately was to get Addy away from these friends who made her eyes light up with pleasure. He wished God could send a sign that he was doing the right thing. After all, God was in the sign-sending business.

Barrett had his usual bored look, and Susan babbled loudly in her familiar way. In a few moments they disappeared into the terminal building. Harry's attention turned to the three men who were talking near their car. He couldn't hear what they said, but there was still something scary about the trio. Two of them puffed on cigarettes while the third twirled his watch chain as he talked. In a few minutes the smokers stubbed out their cigarettes on the ground and started around the hangar.

Unexpectedly to Harry at least, the tallest of the three looked directly at him as he leaned over the turpentine pot. The man's eyes were steely. Harry found himself hoping that the man was simply glancing idly around. Harry lowered his head and began vigorously sloshing the paintbrushes in the turpentine.

A peek at the retreating backs of the men made him freeze. The tall man looked back once more directly at Harry before disappearing around the side of the hangar. This time there was a hint of a smile on the man's lips, but it was the kind of smile that never reached his eyes. It was the kind of smile that sent a chill through a person, and Harry shivered before scrambling up to find Ernie.

"Did you see those three men?" Harry asked his boss, who was inspecting the fuel line on a white monoplane.

"Afraid so," Ernie said with a shake of his head. "They've been around here a lot." He stopped what he was doing to look at Harry. "Mostly in the early mornings or evenings. They fly in and out some with your friend's uncle. Up to no good, if you ask me."

"What do you mean?"

"I can't be sure yet, but I'm keeping my eyes and ears wide open," Ernie replied.

Just then laughter and talking came from the front of the hangar.

"Harry, you in here?" Susan's voice called.

"I'm back here," Harry answered and walked toward the big hangar door.

Susan and Barrett stood just inside the door while Addy lagged behind outside. "Hi there, big boy," Susan said and puckered her lips at him in a pretend kiss before giggling.

Harry swallowed hard and searched his brain for something sensible to say. He knew Susan was teasing, but it was still hard to know how to respond.

Barrett spoke up before Harry could answer Susan. "Why, it's the grease monkey." Harry heard an edge to the young man's voice.

Ignoring Barrett, Harry looked at his cousin. "Hi, Addy. You feeling better?"

Addy stepped out from behind Barrett. "I'm fine. I didn't expect to see you here at the airfield this time of day." She smiled briefly.

"I'm working extra hours to get ready for Lindbergh's visit. Did you know there's going to be a parade, too?" Harry asked.

Susan answered for Addy. "Yes, and I heard that the mayors of both St. Paul and Minneapolis will be riding with Mr. Lindbergh. We're planning to watch from the upstairs window of one of Uncle Marty's businesses. Want to join us, Harry?" Her voice turned silky on the last words.

"No, thanks," Harry said firmly. "I mean, thanks but I'll probably have to help here at the airfield." The last place he wanted to watch the parade was with Susan and Barrett.

"Maybe you'll change your mind," Susan said. "Be sure and ask that cute friend of yours, Nate, if he wants to watch with us. His sister, too, of course."

"Oh, I'll ask." Harry could just hear the argument between Violet and Nate when they heard about the invitation. Nate would think it was a great idea, especially if he knew Susan had called him cute. Violet was likely to take a much dimmer view of the prospect.

"Have you seen the inside of my plane?" Uncle Marty's voice boomed from outside the hangar. "We got it back the other day after they worked it over in Chicago. Come and take a look at it in this other hangar." He walked off, not waiting for them to reply.

Ernie motioned for Harry to go, too, so he whipped off his dirty apron and fell into step beside Addy. He knew that Uncle Marty's plane was back, but it was kept in a small locked hangar. It was the only plane kept under lock and key at the airfield. This was a great chance to see what was so special about that plane.

Harry's eyes grew wide when he looked at the inside of the plane's cabin. He had never seen such a fancy plane before.

"Now these seats here," said Uncle Marty, "have extra stuffing." He pointed to each feature with his cigar. Harry stared at the seats. Dark red material covered them, and they looked like they belonged on a sofa. Tassels and braid hung everywhere, and a soft rug covered the plane's floor.

"Here's the cupboard." Uncle Marty flung open two small doors on the back wall of the passenger cabin.

Harry peered in and saw neat stacks of cups and plates. "Just in case anyone gets hungry during a trip," Uncle Marty said.

"This is really the cat's meow, Uncle," Susan said. "I'm ready to fly off to New York or San Francisco or Paris, now that we know that can be done."

"Whoa, little girl," Uncle Marty said with a deep chuckle. "This plane is for business."

Everyone talked at once as they climbed out of the plane. Barrett was the only one who stood aside, aloof from the others, until Addy walked over to him. Harry couldn't help watching his cousin, even as he listened to Uncle Marty and Susan arguing playfully about a possible destination. Addy grinned up at the young man, who said something under his breath that made her giggle. Harry sighed. Getting her away from Barrett wasn't going to be easy.

Just then Harry saw one of the three men walk around the plane. He must have come out of the terminal while they were inside the airplane. Curious, Harry stepped up near the propeller to see what the man was doing. The short stout man simply stared at the side of the plane for a few moments and then reached up to run a hand over the skin of the fuselage. What on earth?

"Harry, love, where are you?" Susan's loud voice pulled his attention back to the group.

He didn't answer but walked back to stand beside Addy. It was a good thing Nate wasn't here to tease him about being called "love"!

"Uncle Marty is going to take us for a ride in his plane next week if his pilot is available," Susan said sweetly.

She tilted her head at Harry. "Say you'll go with us."

Harry thought of at least five reasons for not going in that many seconds, but he gave only one. "I can't. I'll have to work, but thanks for asking."

"You don't even know which day I was going to say," Susan said, her mouth in a pout.

"I have to work every day until after Lindbergh's visit," Harry said. He realized that, as usual, he had spoken too soon. His mother told him that there was always a perfectly polite way to decline invitations if he thought about it for a moment. He wished he could remember her advice when he needed it.

"I'm sure that Harry would much rather go flying with us than work," said Barrett. "Perhaps you could influence his boss to let him go with us, Uncle Marty."

Harry opened his mouth to answer, but Uncle Marty spoke up first. "First-rate idea, nephew. I'll just step over to the hangar and speak to Ernie."

"No, sir," Harry said more loudly than he intended. Uncle Marty looked back in surprise. "I mean, thank you, but I'll ride some other time if you don't mind. I need to get the work finished."

Uncle Marty nodded. "That's fine, lad. I like a man who takes responsibility." With that he chomped down more firmly on his cigar and walked off toward the cars, where the three men stood waiting.

"Responsibility, my foot," Barrett said. His usually cool expression had changed. He looked almost gleeful. "Mr. Hotshot Harry here doesn't want to go flying with us because he's chicken."

"What are you talking about?" Harry's hair prickled at the sudden attack, but he took a deep breath. Father said that one deep breath could keep a boy out of a world of trouble.

"I know you're scared to fly," Barrett said with a sneer. "Afraid you'll upchuck just like the first time."

"How did you know about that?" Harry's head jerked up, and he stared at Addy. She looked uncomfortable and dropped her eyes. She must have told Barrett about the first time Harry had flown and how sick it made him. Now Barrett knew Harry's deepest fear, that he would never be able to fly again even though he wanted to more than anything.

Harry gazed at Addy until she lifted her chin. He didn't say a word. What could he say? His best friend had betrayed him—and to Barrett, of all people. As he turned away, he saw her chin quiver, but he didn't stop. He kept on walking. The farther away from Addy he could get, the better it would be.

CHAPTER 9

Scissors Happy

Anger and disappointment made Harry's stomach roll as he walked away. Barrett was probably right about his fear of flying, but Addy shouldn't have told the other boy about Harry's first flying experience.

Most of the time Harry laughed about memories of that first trip. After all, he was only ten years old when it happened, but lately he worried that he would never be able to fly without getting airsick. Addy knew about his worries, and now so did Barrett and Susan and anyone they should care to tell. It was downright mean of Addy to tell them. Harry kicked at a single weed that had escaped being pulled. It made him want to get even somehow with his cousin and Barrett.

Ernie looked up when Harry came in and jerked his apron off the hook. The mechanic didn't say anything until they were halfway done replacing the spark plugs in the plane they were working on. "Something's got you riled. What happened?"

Harry shook his head. "Oh, it's nothing." A wrench clattered down inside the engine when Harry dropped it. A few moments later he turned too quickly and knocked a bucket of old oil over.

"Better tell me about this nothing," Ernie said, "before the shop is destroyed."

Harry put down the rag he was using to soak up the spilled oil. It only took a few minutes to tell Ernie the whole story of his first plane ride disaster, his fears about flying, and how Addy had told Barrett.

"Hmm," Ernie said when Harry ran out of breath and story. He wiped his hands slowly on his greasy rag. "As I see it," he said thoughtfully, "this situation has several different sides to it. Now let me say right off that I don't blame you one bit for being peeved at Miss Addy. She shouldn't have talked about something that she knew was more or less a secret."

"I didn't tell her not to tell anyone," Harry admitted with a shrug of his shoulders, "but I thought she knew it was between us." Just hearing Ernie's words helped Harry's anger let up a little.

"No, she was in the wrong, and that Barrett fellow is

just plain mean." Ernie frowned as he jammed his rag back in his pocket. "I'd stay away from that one."

Harry nodded. If he ever saw Barrett again, it would be too soon.

"On the other hand," Ernie continued, "Miss Addy may not have intended to do what she did. Might be that her tongue got in the way of her good sense."

"She never used to be that way."

"People get themselves in all sorts of fixes," Ernie said. "I'd go easy on her until you know the whole story."

"I guess you're right, but I still don't like it."

"Now, as to the other angle of this problem," Ernie said. "The angle where you're worried about being airsick when you fly again."

Harry made a face and shook his head. "I want to fly more than anything in the world, but I'm scared. It's crazy, I know, but there you have it."

Ernie chuckled. "It's not crazy. Lots of pilots get airsick at first."

"They do?"

"They sure do. Most of the time it passes when the old stomach gets used to some ups and downs. Did you like to fly until you got sick that first time?"

"It was terrific," Harry said without hesitation. "I loved it until my stomach started going the opposite way of the rest of my body. Then I had a different opinion."

"Only to be expected," Ernie said, "but I think your next experience will be much better."

"Maybe," Harry said. He was far from convinced, but Ernie had given him a bit of hope that someday he could listen to an airplane's engine from the air rather than on the ground.

After talking to Ernie, Harry changed his mind about wanting to get even with Addy. For now he just wanted to stay away from her. Maybe he'd get over being angry or maybe he'd give her a piece of his mind. He wasn't sure which would happen.

The very next day a note for Harry appeared on the telephone table in the hall while he was at the airfield. It was from Addy and said, "I'm sorry. It was a mistake." Harry stared at the piece of paper for a minute. It was an apology, but it didn't explain anything. He guessed it would have to be enough, for now at least. When all the uproar over Lindbergh's visit was over, he'd try again to pry Addy away from Barrett and his bunch.

The next few days were business as usual at the airfield. With most of the preparations finished at last, Harry guessed that the dignitaries were at home working on their speeches. Decorations would go up at the last minute, so now it was only necessary to keep everything looking neat until the big day. There still seemed to be more people and flights at the airfield, but Harry wasn't sure if it was related to Lindbergh's visit or not. It kept Ernie hopping and Harry, too.

By the time his parents returned from their trips, it no longer seemed absolutely necessary to talk to them about Addy and Barrett, at least not right away. Harry had already decided to work on Addy some more himself when the big celebration was over, so for now he would wait.

On Wednesday afternoon, a week and a half later, Harry got another chance to look at Uncle Marty's plane. It was usually locked up or gone. Ernie said Uncle Marty and his business friends often flew out right after dawn and returned in the early evening or at night. Uncle Marty never asked Ernie to work on his plane, so there was little chance to see it.

But this particular afternoon, the plane sat waiting outside the hangar, its silver paint shining in the hot sun. Harry stopped to look after he took some garbage to the trash pile behind the farthest hangar. It was a beauty of a plane both inside and out. He walked around it to admire the sleek wings.

Odd that the inside seemed small compared to the size of the plane's body. He stood on tiptoe and peeked in the cabin windows at the plush seats and then looked at the outside again. The inside and outside didn't seem to match. The fuel tank took up a certain amount of space behind the cabin, but not this much. Must be some special design.

"Ernie," he asked when he got back to the shop, "have you noticed anything different about Uncle Marty's plane? The size of the inside doesn't match the outside."

"I hadn't noticed," Ernie replied, "but I seldom get much of a look at that plane." He walked out front to squint through the bright sun at the plane that still sat waiting.

"Sometimes these rich guys will redesign their planes, depending on what they use them for. You can put in a bigger fuel tank. Maybe that's what they've done. It's hard to tell from the outside."

"Maybe Uncle Marty had that done while it was in Chicago getting those fancy seats."

"Likely," Ernie agreed. "I'd be interested to know what that bunch is up to."

"Me, too," Harry said as they got back to work. He didn't want to even consider whether or not Barrett might be mixed up with his uncle's business associates.

The following Saturday evening, Mother sent Harry over to Aunt Esther's to return some dress patterns that Mother had borrowed. Aunt Esther took the patterns and invited him to the kitchen for cookies and lemonade.

"It's so hot," she said. "Have a cool drink before you start back. Although I imagine you get a good breeze when you whiz along on your motorcycle."

"At least it dries the sweat on my forehead," Harry said with a laugh. He accepted a glass of lemonade and sat down at the big kitchen table with his aunt. "Is Addy home?"

Aunt Esther's smile faded briefly. "No, she's out. I expect her back soon. She spent the afternoon with Susan. You remember Susan, of course." Aunt Esther glanced at the electric clock that hung on the kitchen wall and frowned. "Actually she's late again. I don't know what's wrong with that girl lately."

Aunt Esther's last words were said softly, almost to herself, so Harry didn't reply. It was obvious that Addy was still causing problems. Now was probably a good time to tell Aunt Esther what he knew about Barrett and Susan and Uncle Marty, but he kept chewing his cookie. He hadn't planned to talk to her today, and the right words didn't immediately come to mind. The cookie stuck in his throat just like the words, and he started coughing.

Aunt Esther jumped up to pound him on the back, and in a few moments he took a drink and croaked, "Thanks, I'm fine now."

"Better slow down," his aunt said with a laugh. "I've never had one of my cookies choke anyone yet."

In between laughing and clearing his throat, Harry heard someone come in the front door. Aunt Esther heard the noise as well and smiled in relief. "Must be Addy," she said. "She'll come back here, I'm sure."

They waited a minute, but Addy didn't appear in the kitchen door. Harry thought he heard footsteps going up the stairs.

"Where'd that girl go?" Aunt Esther wondered. "I'll get her, Harry. I'm sure she'll want to say hello."

Harry wasn't so sure about that, but he didn't say so.

"Addy," Aunt Esther called up the stairs. "Come down, please."

Harry joined his aunt in the front hall. There was no answer from upstairs.

"Addy, where are you?" Aunt Esther called a little louder.

A faint voice floated down the stairs. "I'm here, Mother, but I'm busy."

"Come down anyhow." Aunt Esther's voice was impatient. "Harry's here."

Addy appeared at the top of the stairs just as Uncle Erik came whistling in the front door behind Harry and Aunt Esther.

"Are we having a meeting here in the hallway?" he asked cheerfully. "Hi, there, Harry." He hung up his hat on the coat tree near the door.

"We were just waiting for Addy to come down," Aunt Esther said and smiled at her husband.

All three turned back to the stairs. Addy stood at the top with an odd look on her face. She looked scared yet almost angry, Harry thought.

Aunt Esther gasped.

"Whoa!" Uncle Erik said as he looked at his daughter. "What have you done to yourself?"

Harry looked at his cousin again. Then he saw what her parents had noticed right off. Her brown curls had been cut and combed into a short bobbed style. "Wow!" he said before he could stop himself.

Aunt Esther sank down into a chair that sat near the phone table. "Addy, you've cut your lovely hair. Why?"

Addy looked at the floor in front of her. "I wanted to, that's all."

"That's not a good enough answer," Uncle Erik said and put his hand on Aunt Esther's shoulder. "I know your mother told you that she didn't think bobbed hair was a good idea."

"It's my hair," Addy said and lifted her head. Harry saw that her eyes glowed with defiance. "I wanted to look like all the other girls my age. I wanted to look normal."

Aunt Esther straightened up in her chair. "There's nothing so terrible about bobbed hair. It's the emphasis on appearance that I object to. I think I made myself clear about that. There are more important things in this world to worry about than getting your hair trimmed every month." She shook her head. "At least we could have discussed it."

"Barrett probably talked you into this." The words slipped out before Harry realized that he was talking aloud rather than complaining to himself. He knew it was a major mistake. Addy's head jerked toward him, and if a look could have punched someone, the look she gave him would have put him in the middle of the hallway floor.

"Or probably not, I'm sure," he added hastily. He was annoyed with his cousin, but she was in deep enough trouble already.

"Susan's brother, Barrett?" Aunt Esther asked. "What's he have to do with anything?"

"I thought it was just you and Susan doing things together except for the birthday party," Uncle Erik said. "Barrett's quite a bit older, isn't he?"

"A little," Addy said with a shrug. "He's Susan's brother, so he's around some." She reached up unconsciously to push her hair away from her face.

"According to Harry, this Barrett has quite a bit of influence over you," Aunt Esther said.

Harry wanted to sink out of sight or maybe just slither onto the porch like the snake he was. He wanted Addy's parents to know about Barrett, but not like this.

"Harry doesn't know so much," Addy said. "He's just jealous of Barrett, that's all."

"Is that right, Harry?" Uncle Erik asked. His face was serious, but his voice was kind.

Harry took a deep breath before replying, "No, it's

not, but I shouldn't have said that he had anything to do with Addy getting her hair cut. I don't know if that's true. Maybe it was her own idea."

"I don't know what's worse," Aunt Esther said as she shook her head, "Addy being influenced by someone else or Addy deciding on her own to defy her parents."

Aunt Esther jumped when the phone on the table beside her rang. "Who can that be?" she muttered before picking up the receiver.

"I'm going upstairs to change," Uncle Erik said. "You stay here." He pointed at Addy. "We're not finished with this subject yet."

Aunt Esther pulled a pad of paper out of the table drawer and began taking notes as she talked on the phone.

Addy motioned for Harry to follow her into the living room. He did so reluctantly, afraid of what she would say. All he wanted was to get on his motorcycle and go home.

"Is this how you get even with me?" Addy asked coldly.

"No, it's not. I wouldn't do that." Harry felt a sudden ripple of guilt. He had thought about getting even with her for telling Barrett about the flying, but speaking out this evening was an accident, wasn't it?

"I didn't mean to say anything. It just came out. Probably the same way you told Barrett about me getting airsick." He stared at Addy until she looked down. "Why in the world did you get your hair bobbed anyway, when you knew your parents would be upsct?"

"I just wanted to do something different, something fun and a little crazy," Addy said and touched a hand to her hair.

"Crazy is the right word. You're in for it now."

"It wouldn't be so bad if you hadn't mentioned Barrett."

"Maybe so, but Addy, Barrett is trouble, worse trouble than you're in with your parents. And I'm not so sure about Uncle Marty and his business associates." Harry stopped talking to shake his head. "I wish you'd stay away from them."

"They're my friends," Addy said hotly. "I can't just tell them to go away because they make my cousin nervous. I don't want to do that, and I won't." She glared at Harry. "Of course, who knows what my parents will make me do now that they think I'm being badly influenced, thanks to you."

Harry wished he could say he was sorry. He even opened his mouth, but the words wouldn't come out. He wasn't sorry that her parents at least knew that Addy's new friendship with Susan included an older brother. It wasn't the whole story, but maybe it would help.

A few moments later, Uncle Erik came downstairs, and Aunt Esther finished her phone conversation. They both appeared in the living-room door.

"I better go now," Harry said. Addy would have to deal with her parents, and he didn't want to hear how she did it. He was afraid he wouldn't like what he heard.

Ernie's Surprise

"You're awfully quiet, Harry," Mother said the next morning at breakfast. "Is something wrong?" She had just placed a Sunday morning breakfast of pancakes in front of him. The sweet maple smell made Harry's mouth water.

"No, I'm all right," he replied as he attacked the pancakes with his fork. "I'm just thinking about stuff." The scene at Addy's last night was still fresh in his mind.

Mother sat down at her place and smiled at Harry as she poured syrup over her steaming pancakes. "Don't forget that God is interested in all kinds of stuff, as you call it. He'll help you figure things out if you ask."

Harry nodded. Sometimes he did forget to pray, even though he knew it was the right thing to do.

"I talked to Esther this morning," Mother said. "Addy came home with bobbed hair last night, which caused quite an uproar."

"Aunt Esther didn't want her to get her hair cut?" Gloria asked.

"No, she didn't. At least not without talking about it," Mother replied.

"What's wrong with bobbed hair?" Father asked. "Gloria's is bobbed."

"It's not the haircut that's the problem," Mother answered. "The problem is that Addy got it cut against her parents' wishes."

"Why would Aunt Esther and Uncle Erik care about bobbed hair?" Gloria asked and reached for some more pancakes.

"They don't want Addy putting too much attention on her appearance. They want her to keep her mind on more important things," Mother said.

"That's a lot to expect from a fourteen-year-old girl," Father said.

"I know," Mother said with a sigh. "I'm afraid that we haven't heard the end of Addy's problems. Sometimes that household is just much too serious for a child."

Harry listened but didn't speak up. Aunt Esther must not have mentioned to Mother that he had been present last night when Addy's haircut was discovered. He opened his mouth to say so, but then everyone was getting up from the table. It was time to leave for church, and as was usual with the Allertons, there was no time to spare. Especially since Fred had dripped syrup on his shirt, requiring a hurried trip upstairs for a change.

Addy and her family arrived at church just as the song leader was announcing the first hymn. They slid in at the end of their regular pew, so Harry only got a brief look at his cousin. She stared straight ahead with her chin in the air. Harry had to poke Fred, who had leaned way out to look at Addy's new hairstyle. As little as Harry cared about hairstyles, he could see that Addy's looked fine. It made her appear older, but other than that, she just looked like most of the young women and girls sitting around the church. It was hard to understand what all the fuss was about.

Harry thought about Addy while everyone sang hymns and listened to announcements. It didn't seem so long ago that he was causing all the trouble with his practical jokes. Addy had put up with a lot of aggravation from him. He wished he could do something to help her now, but what? He had tried lots of things, but nothing seemed to work. She was still friends with Barrett and Susan, in spite of his efforts to change her mind about them. It seemed hopeless.

The preacher boomed out the opening line of his sermon, "Put your hope in God and nothing else."

Harry's eyes opened wide. Maybe God was sending him a message. "Pray about this, Harry Allerton, and I will help you." He could do that, and maybe God would make it clear whether or not he should tell his parents or his aunt and uncle everything he knew about Uncle Marty and Barrett or whether he should keep on trying to help Addy himself. He hoped God worked fast.

Final preparations for the big day of Lindbergh's visit got started at the airfield that week when the army hauled in some big artillery guns to fire for the celebration. Harry found himself pulling more weeds and trimming grass that had grown back since the first round of clean-up several weeks ago. He spent one whole day washing windows in the terminal building that he had washed once already.

Excited as he was about the celebration and as much as he wanted everything to look just right, he still thought the extra window washing excessive. Harry thought it unlikely that Charles Lindbergh cared a bit about plants or clean windows. His mind was probably in the sky.

There were extra people at the airfield off and on all week. Some of them were clearly related to Lindbergh's visit, but others seemed extra. Harry had seen a couple of men walking behind the hangars and looking in each plane that was parked. Another day he saw the same two men with a third, talking to the terminal manager.

"Are those two guys here because of the celebration?" Harry asked Ernie late on Friday afternoon. Ernie had burned his hand on Wednesday, so he was mostly watching Harry do the work as they serviced a mail plane. He jabbed his finger in the direction of the men who stood in front of Uncle Marty's hangar.

"I'm not sure," Ernie admitted and straightened up to look at the men. "They could be some kind of security, I guess. Maybe the mayor's wife has hired a little extra help. She probably doesn't trust the police department."

"I'm surprised she's not doing the security herself," Harry said with a shake of his head. He had just finished more cleaning at the request of the mayor's wife.

Ernie chuckled. "It will all be over soon, if we can live that long."

"I can't wait for Tuesday," Harry said. "Do you think we'll be able to get close to Mr. Lindbergh? There'll be tons of people here."

"I should think so. I've already been in touch with Charlie to tell him we'll be watching for him," Ernie said.

Harry was silent for a moment before words poured out. "What do you mean? How could you get in touch with Lindbergh? Are you kidding me?"

"So many questions," Ernie said with a grin. He tossed a bolt into a can on the workbench. "I sent him a telegram. That was easy as pie. He telegraphed back that he'd be watching for us."

"Why would he do that when he doesn't even know us?" Harry felt confused, but at the same time a buzz of excitement ran through him.

"Because he does know us, or at least he knows me. We flew together back in his barnstorming days. That was before we both got some sense and gave up that dangerous sport."

"But you never told me," Harry said. "Why didn't you tell me that you actually knew the most famous pilot in the world?"

"It didn't come up," Ernie said. "Besides, I didn't want to disappoint you if I couldn't get in touch with him ahead of time. Who knows, he might not have remembered me."

"I think you could have told me anyhow," Harry said. He was quiet for a moment. "So you're saying that not only can I see Charles Lindbergh, I might get to meet him?" Suddenly Harry felt a strong urge to dance around and shout his pleasure.

"Short of some major hitch in the plans, you will indeed be meeting Lucky Lindy. In my telegram I told him that I had a young mechanic friend I wanted him to meet."

Harry felt like he needed to sit down. He was the one who was lucky, no doubt about it.

"Now that we have this all ironed out, let's get back to work. The pilot of this mail plane will be back anytime, and we better have it ready." Ernie stuck his unbandaged hand into the engine in an effort to make a final adjustment. "Did your mother say it was all right for you to spend the night tonight to help me with those extra mail flights?"

Harry pulled his mind out of the clouds, where it had been soaring with Lucky Lindy, and back to the shop with Ernie. "She said it would be fine. I almost forgot. She sent a pie for us to eat. It's in my bag." Occasionally Ernie slept over at the airfield if there were extra mail flights scheduled to come in late or very early. There were a couple cots in a storage room at the back of the shop. This time he had asked Harry to sleep over and help.

"Your mother is a jewel of a woman," Ernie said. "If I didn't have this banged-up hand, you wouldn't have to stay, but I'm glad your parents agreed."

Harry nodded and attempted to place his attention

firmly on the engine in front of him. It wasn't easy when all he could think of was meeting Charles Lindbergh next Tuesday afternoon.

It was almost eleven o'clock that night before Harry got to crawl into his cot in the storage room. A breeze blew in the tiny window, but it was still hot, and Harry lay awake for a while, waiting to cool off. In minutes Ernie snored softly from the other cot. It would have been hard to get to sleep, even without the heat, because Harry's mind was full of the upcoming visit. He grinned in the dark as he thought about meeting Charles Lindbergh. Wait till Addy heard about this. His grin faded as he remembered that Addy was probably still angry with him.

A noise outdoors interrupted his gloomy thoughts. At first he thought it was just the usual kind of noise that a person heard at night when he was awake and everyone else was asleep. But then he heard the sound again, a scraping and then a thump. Now it was louder and more distinct. He raised his head off the pillow and tilted it. A faint voice drifted in the window. Someone was out there!

Harry looked over at Ernie, who still slept soundly. He listened for a few moments, but didn't hear anything else. Quietly he sat up and slipped his feet into his shoes. He had slept in his pants, so he was dressed. With a last glance at Ernie, Harry tiptoed out the storage room door into the hangar. He'd look for himself before waking his boss.

He looked up and down the double row of hangars that sat at the head of the airstrip. Moonlight outlined the fronts of the buildings dimly, but no movement caught his eye. He stood still, listening. At first he heard only the crickets that chirped from the trees and brush behind the hangars, but then a single voice and a second floated to him on the breeze. He twisted his head, trying to find the direction of the voices. Another bump accompanied by louder voices helped pinpoint the sounds to the end of the row of hangars. The sounds were coming from Uncle Marty's hangar, or at least from that general area.

Harry walked quietly toward the source of the noises, keeping in the shadows as much as possible. Eyes strained forward, he darted softly across the patches of moonlight between the hangar buildings. It wouldn't do to get caught right now. Finally he reached the last hangar before Uncle Marty's. Tucked carefully into the shadow, he peered around the edge of the building. There was nothing in front of Uncle Marty's hangar, not a sign of anyone or anything, but the big doors were open and the plane sat inside in darkness. He knew that Uncle Marty and one of his business associates had flown in earlier. He was sure that the doors had been locked as usual after that.

A scrap of conversation reached his ears, but he couldn't understand the faint words. They seemed to be coming from behind Uncle Marty's hangar. Staying in the shadows, Harry scooted around to the back edge of the building. At first he was disappointed because he saw nothing but trees and brush and an old rutted lane that wound out of sight over a little hill.

Then a light bobbed briefly among the trees. Another blinked farther away. At least two people with some kind of lights, probably lanterns, were walking down the old lane. Harry watched as the lights disappeared over the hill. Before he could move from his hiding place, a voice that was much closer startled him.

"I'll get the doors."

Someone without a light stood beside the back of Uncle Marty's hangar. Harry could only see the outline of a person in the moonlight. That person walked around to the front of the hangar, and Harry heard the big doors swing shut. In a moment the figure reappeared behind the building and started down the lane. Another voice spoke out of the darkness.

"Is everything shut up?"

"Yes, and locked up, too," came the reply.

"Let's get out of here before those clumsy oafs drop anything else."

A lantern flickered on, and Harry saw the two figures meet in the lane. Without another word they disappeared over the hill, and in a few minutes Harry heard the sound of a car engine starting.

Harry didn't move. He just stared at the crest of the hill. At last he turned and walked back through the darkness toward the shop. That voice, the one who accused others of being clumsy oafs, was all too familiar. It sounded like Barrett. Harry was practically certain it was the older boy. What was he doing at the airfield in the middle of the night, and who was with him?

Harry climbed back into his cot without waking Ernie. There was nothing to be done tonight, and Harry wanted to think this all through before telling anyone what he had seen. The night's events played endlessly in his mind until exhaustion took over, and he fell asleep.

It was midmorning Saturday before Harry had a spare moment to tell Ernie about the previous night's visitors. Mail planes had flown in early with engine problems that had to be fixed right away. With Ernie largely unable to use his right hand, Harry worked on the engines while Ernie occasionally looked over his shoulder. At last the planes were off, and Harry led Ernie behind Uncle Marty's hangar to show him where he had seen the lights and people.

"They weren't careful about making tracks," Ernie said as he looked at the grassy lane. The grass was beaten down, and here and there a footprint showed clearly in a dusty bare spot. "I wonder what they were up to?" The mechanic stared up the lane to the crest of the small hill.

"Where does this road go, anyhow?" Harry asked. Something had made him not tell Ernie that he'd recognized Barrett's voice. It seemed right to wait until he was absolutely sure that it had been Barrett with the lantern.

"I think it winds around back there and finally comes out near old Fort Snelling," Ernie answered. "Hard to say what they were doing. They probably didn't even know anyone was here at the airfield last night. Your motorcycle was in the hangar where our shop is, and I got a ride yesterday since I can't drive with this old hurt hand."

It was a puzzle and not one Harry could solve right away. He promised himself that as soon as Ernie was back to normal and Lindbergh's visit was over, he'd explore down that lane and see what he could see. Meanwhile, he didn't know what, if anything, to do about

Barrett's role. Addy's friendship with Susan and Barrett had turned out to have more knots than a tangled up fishing line, and Harry didn't know what to do to untangle everything.

That evening when Harry got home, he found that the family was going to Addy's house for dinner. He was tired and dirty and just wanted to stretch out on the living-room rug and listen to the radio, but his parents told him that he could do that in Aunt Esther's living room. Too tired to argue, he took a bath and changed clothes. Uncle Erik's radio was top-notch, so maybe that would be fine. Harry hadn't seen Addy since last Sunday and hadn't talked to her since the bobbed hair episode. He wasn't sure how she would act toward him, but he had to find out sometime. Tonight might as well be the night.

Addy was her usual quiet self at dinner except for laughing with Fred, who sat beside her at the table. She had said hi to Harry when he arrived, but that was all there was time for since dinner was ready. It was a relief to know that she didn't intend to completely ignore him. Knowing that let him enthusiastically eat three pieces of fried steak and a double helping of mashed potatoes and gravy before getting full.

After dinner, Harry sat on the floor against Uncle Erik's big chair and listened to the radio for a while. *Amos and Andy* was on, which was always funny. Addy had disappeared as soon as Fred curled up on the sofa and went to sleep. When the orchestra came on the radio, Harry decided to retreat to the front porch. He hesitated when he saw Addy sitting in the porch swing, lit only by the soft glow of the street light. He took a deep breath and pushed open the front screen door. Time to talk to his cousin.

"Hi," he said and sat down in a chair near the swing. "What are you doing?"

"Just swinging and thinking," Addy replied. "That's all."

They sat in silence for a few minutes. Harry watched lightning bugs twinkle in the front yard while the crickets made their usual racket.

"How's your job going?" Addy asked at last.

"Fine. I love it," Harry answered. "I didn't get to tell you yet about Ernie knowing Charles Lindbergh." He told her all about the promised introduction when Lindbergh arrived that Tuesday.

"How exciting," Addy said. "You'll be famous yourself at school if you get to meet him."

"I suppose so," Harry said. "Say, you can come, too. I'm sure Ernie would be glad to introduce you the same as me."

"That would be terrific. Maybe I'll do that." Addy sounded almost as excited as he was.

"Speaking of excitement," Harry said, making a quick decision, "there was something going on at the airfield last night. Something I can't figure out." Before he could think better of it, he told Addy all about the sounds and lights. She listened in silence.

"The thing is," Harry said finally, "I'm almost positive that the last voice I heard was Barrett's."

"Barrett's?" Addy said sharply and planted her feet on the porch floor to stop the gently rocking swing. "Why do you think that? Did you see him?"

"No," Harry admitted. "I didn't see anyone clearly, but it sounded exactly like his voice."

"It could have been someone who sounded like him."

"True, but I don't think it was."

"Well, I think you're wrong," Addy said flatly. "Why would he be at that airfield in the middle of the night?" She jumped up from the swing, banged in the screen door, and ran up the stairs. Harry heard her bedroom door slam in the distance.

"Why indeed would Barrett be at the airfield in the middle of the night?" Harry repeated softly to himself. "Why indeed?"

CHAPTER 11

A Kink in the Plans

The more Harry thought about Friday night, the more certain he was that the voice belonged to Barrett. There wasn't time right now to poke around for answers, but Harry vowed to start looking as soon as the excitement at the airfield was over. Addy might know more than she was saying.

Monday morning the airfield swarmed with workers and reporters and city officials. The workers fixed ropes to control the huge crowds of people expected to show up on Tuesday. Soldiers checked and rechecked the big artillery guns that sat well off to one side of the field. Everything that could be done to make Charles Lindbergh's visit perfect was done—and then some.

City officials walked here and there, stopping occasionally to issue an order, but mostly talking to each other and to reporters. Ernie's hand was better, so Harry had been loaned out again for decorating duty. All day long, people ordered Harry about as he strung ropes of banners and stuck small American flags everywhere. They were bossy, but they were almost as excited as Harry was even if their reason for being excited was different. Unlike the adults, making Minneapolis a shining example of civic pride wasn't Harry's goal. He just wanted to be standing beside Ernie when Lindbergh's plane came flying out of the clouds.

Tuesday morning was sunny and hot even at seven when Harry arrived at the airfield on his motorcycle. Mother promised to call Addy to tell her to meet him at noon if she wanted to be there with Ernie and Harry to meet Mr. Lindbergh. There wasn't a lot left to do except marvel at the number of people who streamed into the airfield's parking lots and eventually spilled over onto the grassy sides of the runway. Open cars ready for the parade lined the edge of the field, and by eleven, city officials in their fancy suits and hats began to arrive. Soldiers stood guard around the artillery guns, and policemen were everywhere.

Even Ernie had dressed up for the big day. Not a bit of grease streaked his face, and the dirty rag that usually poked out of his back pocket was gone.

Harry kept his eyes open for Addy while he carried more chairs out for officials to sit on in the shade of the terminal building. Uncle Erik had a newspaper pass that should get Addy and him past the crowds and policemen who formed a human line around the terminal building.

There was a false alarm a little after eleven when a plane appeared overhead. The crowd cheered and the officials scrambled for their appointed places, but it turned out to be the advance man for Mr. Lindbergh. His early arrival was timed to check the security arrangements. He assured everyone that Lindbergh would arrive promptly at two o'clock as scheduled.

Noon came with no sign of Addy. Harry found a clean spot in the shop to sit and eat a sandwich that he had brought in his lunch bag. Excitement kept him from tasting a single bite. He could hardly keep from going outside to look at the skies, even though he knew that it would be a couple hours before Charles Lindbergh's plane appeared.

"Harry," someone called. It was Uncle Erik. Beside him walked a man with a large camera. "Your big day?" The pair came through the hangar to where Harry sat at the back of the shop.

Harry nodded with a smile. "Where's Addy?"

"I don't know," Uncle Erik said, frowning. "Am I supposed to know?"

"I thought she was coming to the airfield with you to meet Mr. Lindbergh," Harry said, "but maybe she decided to watch the parade with Nate and Violet."

"I left early for my office, and she didn't telephone me there," Uncle Erik said. "She must be with the others."

Harry nodded again. He was disappointed. Addy was the one person he wanted to share this exciting day with.

Uncle Erik and his photographer hurried off when someone hollered for them. Harry shoved his empty lunch bag onto the shelf. Things never seemed to go as planned lately, but he wasn't going to let Addy's absence spoil anything.

People and cars milled together in big clumps in the parking lots and in front of the hangars. With horns honking, drivers inched their cars through the people, who paid little attention to the vehicles. Everyone wanted to be on the front row.

Harry walked across the open area in front of the hangars on one last errand for the mayor's wife. Harry glanced at the umbrella he had retrieved from her car. It didn't look like rain, but maybe she wanted to be ready for anything. He was almost back to the terminal building when a car crossed in front of him, going much faster than was safe with a sea of people still wandering around.

Harry stopped short with a bark of surprise as the car almost ran over his toes. When he raised his gaze to glare at the back of the careless driver's head, he looked through the side window of the car directly into Addy's white face. Her eyes looked huge and frightened and didn't seem to focus on Harry. She turned her head before he could move to attract her attention.

In a moment the car disappeared through the crowd. Harry followed, trying to make his way through the bystanders and stay alongside the car. He didn't know what was going on, but he aimed to find out. Addy's scared face was not the face of someone joining a celebration for a famous pilot.

Harry reached the end of the car, but before he could

yank the back car door open, the vehicle shot forward. The crowd had cleared, and the driver made for the lane that ran behind Uncle Marty's hangar. Harry ran down the lane, following the car as it plunged over the bumpy road. The back end of the car heaved up and down, but the driver only drove faster. At last Harry stopped and watched helplessly as the car disappeared over the little hill, leaving only a haze of dust behind.

Something was terribly wrong. Harry was sure of that. He needed help, but as he turned back to the scene on the airfield, he knew that might be hard to come by. Policemen were everywhere, but would they help him? Somehow he doubted they would respond immediately to his tale of a scared friend hauled off in a car down an old road. Ernie would, of course, but Harry didn't even know where his boss was right now. Valuable time could be lost just searching for him. It seemed more important to find out where Addy was going if that was possible. That he could do himself.

He pushed through the crowd to the shop to get his motorcycle. In less than a minute he roared down the lane after Addy. He had shoved the umbrella in the arms of a wide-eyed little boy and told him to take it to the mayor's wife. Hopefully the boy would obey.

Harry dodged the ruts in the road and was quickly over the rise. The road, which was little more than two tracks with grass grown up all around, wound up and down through trees and brush. Harry went as fast as he dared, hoping that the vehicle might have stopped along this road. He watched carefully for forks in the main trail, but brush closed in below and treetops above until he felt like he was riding through a long green tunnel.

He rode for more than a mile before the green tunnel opened out into a large meadow. A bright light that might have been a reflection flashed on the other side of the field. Harry quickly killed his motor. He heard an engine roar briefly and then stop. After pushing the cycle up under a tree, he peeked between the leaves and saw the dim outline of a car across the meadow. Faint voices reached him, but he couldn't make out any words.

Harry hesitated. He thought that was the car he had seen. What other car would be back here in the woods that bordered the meadow? What to do now? All he could think of was to get close enough to make sure Addy was all right. If he stayed at the edge of the woods, he should be able to sneak up on whoever was across the field with his cousin. He pushed his motorcycle back a little farther in the shadows under the trees and began to make his way around the edge to the far side, pushing the heavy cycle.

He was more than halfway there when he reached a small creek that curved up by the tree line and was bordered on both sides by rocky ditches. Standing by the creek, Harry sized up the situation. He'd have to leave the cycle on this side. He hated to leave his means of escape so far away, but there was no way to get the cycle over the creek, and going around meant venturing into the open meadow. He didn't want to chance that.

He fixed the cycle on its stand, checked his pocket for the screwdriver he sometimes carried, and headed out. The screwdriver was as close to a weapon as he could manage.

He wasn't sure it would be of any help, but it couldn't hurt. Harry climbed over the rocks and across the creek as quietly as possible.

In minutes Harry was close enough to the other side to see for sure that the car was the same one he had seen earlier. It was parked alongside an old building that was little more than a shack. Behind the shack sat a smaller stone building. The structures were in a small clearing at the edge of the big meadow. Tall trees grew behind them, and another overgrown road disappeared through an opening in the trees.

Harry ran from tree to tree in the shadows as he worked his way closer to the two buildings. At first there was no sign of anyone, but as he darted behind the big bush nearest the car, Harry heard the door of the shack burst open.

"What are we supposed to do with her now?" The loud words carried easily to Harry's hiding place. He moved his head a few inches and saw through the leaves that a tall man was pushing Addy in front of him as they walked toward the car. It was one of the men Harry had seen at the airfield a few weeks ago.

"Beats me, but we couldn't leave her at the house like old Romeo wanted to," a second man growled. Harry saw him jerk his thumb back. Through the doorway of the shack, a third man came. It was Barrett! Gone was his usual bored expression. He looked worried. Harry pulled back for a moment. If Barrett was scared, then there must be real trouble here.

"If you idiots had left her at the house like I wanted, we wouldn't have a hostage to deal with," Barrett said in disgust. He stood by the car, his hands jammed in the pockets of his neatly pressed pants.

"Sure, Mr. Fancy-pants," the short man said, "so she could hop right up and call the police or the Feds. No, sir, she should have minded her own business. One more load of this premium whiskey is all we have coming since the Feds are closing in. Get it in, get it loaded, and get out of here. Sounds simple, but not with this gal."

"I'm not letting some nosy girl cheat me out of the pretty penny this load will bring," the tall man said. "The money will get us out of this boring town and back to Chicago, where there's some real action. We were lucky to find this meadow to fly out of when the Feds came breathing down our necks at the airfield. No, sir, this caper is going down the way it's supposed to."

Bootleggers! Harry took a deep breath. One of the voices sounded like the one he heard with Barrett last Friday night behind Uncle Marty's hangar. Maybe he should have guessed that Uncle Marty's business associates were mixed up in the illegal liquor trade, but he hadn't wanted to think that about jovial Uncle Marty. But now it seemed that Barrett and Susan's uncle was involved—he might even be the boss. Harry moved carefully around the back of the bush where he was hiding. Addy was blocked from his view until he darted across the few open feet to a different bush.

Now he could see her. Surprisingly she stood tall with her chin stuck out. Harry knew she must be terrified, but she didn't show it. The two bootleggers stood on either side of her while they talked.

The sound of a car engine made Harry duck down lower before peering through the leaves again. A car had pulled into the clearing from the road he had seen earlier. The doors burst open, and Uncle Marty stomped across the clearing, followed by yet another man.

"What in the world is going on?" Uncle Marty demanded. "Why is this girl here? Have you all gone crazy?" In his excitement, Uncle Marty almost lost the cigar that hung out of the side of his mouth.

"She knows too much," the tall man said. "We didn't know what else to do with her."

"I can think of a hundred things to do with her that don't include bringing her along," Uncle Marty snapped. "And Barrett, what are you doing here? You know better."

Harry saw Barrett shake his head briefly and shrug his shoulders, but the boy didn't say anything.

"Joe-Joe," Uncle Marty said to the short man, "you and Hank here are morons. If the Feds weren't hot on our trail already, they will be as soon as this girl doesn't show up for dinner."

Harry watched as Uncle Marty walked over to stand in front of Addy. He strained to hear what the man said to his cousin. "I'm sorry as I can be that you got mixed up in this, little lady."

"What's going to happen to me now?" Addy said in a steady voice that carried easily to Harry's ears.

Uncle Marty shook his head and frowned. "I'm not sure about that. Not sure at all. This bunch better have some ideas." He glared at the two men he had called

Joe-Joe and Hank. "For now you can relax in the rock hut. It'll be cool there."

He turned to the man who had arrived with him. "Al, get a couple of rugs out of the car and fix her a spot in the hut. Then post a lookout, which will have to be you. We don't need anything else going wrong. All of the hullabaloo with Lindbergh's visit should have made this last pickup a cinch, but no, these two have turned it into a kidnapping."

He stomped off toward the shed, muttering and chewing on his cigar. At the door he turned again. "Barrett, see that she's comfortable and get yourself in here."

Harry watched as Al did as ordered. Barrett stood where he was for a long time. Addy yanked her shoulder away when Al put his hand on it to guide her toward the hut.

"Aren't you the feisty one?" Al said with a nasty laugh and grabbed her anyway.

"Don't touch me," Addy said and pulled away from him again. "I'm going."

"Your girlfriend isn't as sweet as we thought, Barrett, old pal."

"Shut your mouth! I'm not his girlfriend, and I never was." Addy practically spat the words out. She gave Al a final shove and stalked off to the stone hut.

Harry wiggled around in his nest under the bush. He measured the distance to the hut in his mind. Maybe he could reach the back of it without being seen. Several minutes passed as he planned how to make a run for it. Before he could go, the shed door flew open. He dropped back down into the bush.

"Be sure and put the lanterns in the meadow," Uncle Marty said.

"Will do, boss," Joe-Joe said.

"What about the gal?" Al called. He slammed the hut door and came toward the group.

"Where's Barrett?" Uncle Marty asked.

"In there with the gal," Al replied with a gritty laugh. "She's not too happy with your nephew. Probably in there chewing him up and spittin' him out."

"That girl is putting a kink in our plans," Uncle Marty said and gave his cigar a vicious chomp.

"What you doing with her?" Al asked again.

"Nothing good, that's for sure." Uncle Marty yanked open the car door. Harry crawled as close to the edge of the bush as he dared. He had to hear what Uncle Marty said.

"We'll have to take her to Chicago and lay low until we can get the operation here shut down." He frowned at the others. "Then we'll see about letting her go. Don't know if that will be possible. Have to wait and see."

A cold chill spilled over Harry as he knelt in the bush. They were taking Addy to Chicago! Fear made his mouth go dry. They might let her go, if it was possible. He crawled back a few feet to sit under a big tree. He took some deep breaths and closed his eyes.

For the first time since this wild chase had started, he prayed. With his whole heart and soul, he prayed that Addy would be safe. He prayed that somehow this horrible day, which should have been the best day of his life, would end with Addy safe and sound. But as he huddled under the tree, Harry wasn't sure how that was going to happen.

125

CHAPTER 12
Fixing Things

The door of the stone hut opened with a loud screech. Harry moved to see who came out. Barrett came out the door but turned and went back in.

"I didn't know what they planned, Addy." Barrett's voice was loud as he appeared in the door again. His usual cool way of speaking was gone. "I said I was sorry."

It must be explanation time for Barrett. Harry wished he could hear all of what the young man was saying, but

Barrett had turned his back. Harry could only watch to see what would happen next. In a moment or two Barrett stomped out and across the clearing to the shack. With a fearsome screech, the door slammed shut from the inside. Harry couldn't keep from grinning. Addy still had spunk. His grin faded as he thought again of the bootleggers and Chicago. What could he do?

Harry looked around the clearing. Everyone had gone in the shed but the man they called Joe-Joe, and he sat on an upturned bucket in front of the stone hut, smoking a cigarette. Uncle Marty had driven away, leaving the three men and Barrett. Addy wasn't locked in, but there was no way for her to get out without being seen.

Harry stood up. Going from the shadows of one tree to the next, he worked his way to the edge of the clearing and moved closer to the back of the hut. He stopped when he could still see Joe-Joe puffing on his cigarette in front of the hut but could also see the back and side of the little building.

There was a window! Harry almost burst out with a relieved laugh before he noticed how high the small opening was. Too high to reach without something to stand on, the window looked more like a hole where the stones had crumbled. How could he get Addy out of there without attracting attention from Joe-Joe?

Harry moved back into the woods a few feet to sit on a fallen tree and think. Maybe he should go back the way he had come and get help at the airfield. He wouldn't be able to start the motorcycle right away for fear of being heard. If the bootleggers knew they had been watched, they might run and take Addy with them. So he'd have to walk and push the cycle at first.

But what if Uncle Marty returned and decided to take Addy off somewhere else? The whole bunch might be long gone before Harry could get back with help. Harry chewed his bottom lip and looked at the sun. It must be almost two o'clock. He had no more than thought about the time when a faint engine sound buzzed somewhere above him. At first he ignored it, but the sound grew steadily louder.

He glanced idly up through the tree leaves before he remembered. That buzz must be Charles Lindbergh flying into Wold-Chamberlain Airfield. Flying in to be honored by the city and to meet his old friend Ernie, who wanted to introduce him to a young mechanic. Harry forgot where he was for an instant and jumped up. Dashing forward to the edge of the trees, he peered skyward. The drone of the engine came from directly over the meadow. There it was, glinting in the afternoon sun, the *Spirit of St. Louis*. Harry watched as the plane slowly flew out of sight.

He stared at the spot where the plane had vanished from view. A wave of sorrow flowed over him. He had wanted so much to see Lindbergh, to meet the aviator who had claimed the whole world's attention.

He shook his head to clear it. There was no time now for regrets. Addy was in desperate trouble, and it was up to him to rescue her. He thought of all the times he had considered telling Aunt Esther and Uncle Erik what he knew about Barrett and Uncle Marty but hadn't. If he had told them, in spite of Addy's anger, would she be shut up in a hut in the woods now guarded by a crook named Joe-Joe? Probably not.

Harry sat in the grass where he could see the clearing and waited and planned. Some loud booms echoed far off, and he realized that it was the artillery guns welcoming Lindbergh. Once he thought he heard cheering in the distance, but it might have only been the wind.

After thinking up a dozen plans to rescue Addy and discarding each one, Harry settled on one idea. It wasn't foolproof, but it might work. Now he had to settle down and wait for dark and pray that the bootleggers wouldn't make their move before then.

Stretched out on the soft grass, he rested his head on a raised tree root. He poked gently at some beetles on a nearby rotten stump with the screwdriver that fell out of his pocket when he lay down. The woods were so peaceful that he could almost forget why he was here.

The afternoon passed. The only movement came when Hank appeared to take Joe-Joe's place on guard. Harry didn't bother to get up but watched the two from his spot. They barely exchanged words, so Harry guessed that nothing had changed.

At last the sun dipped below the trees in the west. For once Harry was glad that the days were shorter at the end of August. It would mean less time to wait before he could get to work.

Harry judged it to be almost seven o'clock when the sound of voices came from the front of the shack. He couldn't see exactly what was happening, but in a minute he saw Al and Joe-Joe with lanterns in their hands walking across the meadow. He remembered what Uncle Marty had said about putting the lanterns out, but what were they for? The two men placed the lanterns at what looked like four corners of a big skinny rectangle.

Before he could figure out their actions, an answer flew out of the sky. Al and Joe-Joe had barely reached the clearing again when an airplane swooped down through the dusk and landed in the meadow, neatly positioned between the lanterns.

In the near darkness, Harry crept closer to the buildings. The airplane taxied up and stopped at the edge of the meadow. It appeared the bootleggers were using an airplane to haul their liquor. Were they bringing the illegal booze into Minneapolis or taking it out? Harry's thoughts tumbled over each other as he tried to think how this might affect his plan to rescue Addy. A suspicion wiggled its way into his brain. Maybe they planned to take Addy to Chicago in the airplane. The more he thought about it, the more certain he was that it must be the plan.

Scrambling up from his hiding place, Harry moved closer to the stone hut. There was less time than he had thought. Now that the time had come, he was afraid his idea wouldn't work. How would he get Addy's attention through the hole in the hut without attracting the guard? He had intended to wait until the guard was asleep, but the bootleggers might be long gone with Addy in the plane before anyone slept.

A car roared into the clearing again. Harry saw lanterns and heard voices.

"I see you made it," Uncle Marty boomed out of the

darkness. "Hope the stuff you brought is the real McCoy. We've got a peck of trouble here. At least I want to make my profit on this shipment."

An unfamiliar voice vouched for the quality of the liquor. It must be the pilot. The lanterns moved toward the shed. It looked like all of the bootleggers disappeared through the shed door. Was there a guard in front, or had they forgotten? It didn't matter. This was the time for Harry to make his move.

It was fully dark, and only the stars twinkled above. No moon lit up the clearing yet, and Harry moved as silently as he could to the cars. Quickly he slithered on his back under the rear of Uncle Marty's car. In seconds he had located the fuel line and unscrewed the clamp with his screwdriver. With a sharp jerk, he pulled the fuel line loose and dodged the spurt of gasoline that splashed near his head. He rolled out from under Uncle Marty's car and crawled over to the other one. There he repeated his actions.

Now he had to fix the airplane. He hadn't planned for this, but it had to be done. With the airplane disabled as well as the cars, the crooks would be slowed down if not stopped. He paused in the deeper shadows by Uncle Marty's car and looked around. The airplane was several yards out into the meadow. It might be dark, but if someone was watching, a person running could be seen. Also he wasn't sure if he could get into the engine of the airplane without making some noise. Still there was no sign of anyone in the clearing. They must not have noticed yet that no one was on guard.

Harry took a deep breath and ran through the tall grass at the edge of the meadow. Reaching the far side of the airplane, he stopped and waited. No shout of discovery rang out. So far so good. He realized that this was Uncle Marty's plane with the fancy seats. Now it seemed clear why the inside was small when compared with the outside of the plane. The extra room was some kind of cargo space for carrying bootlegged liquor.

Harry inched the service panel off as quietly as possible. One loud scrape made him catch his breath, but a moment's listening convinced him that the crooks were still inside the shed. He yanked several spark plug wires out and tossed them as far away in the tall grass as possible. This plane wasn't moving anytime soon.

Now he ran directly to the side of the stone hut. "Addy, Addy," he whispered toward the opening above. He waited a moment before calling again. At last there was a sound from inside.

"Harry, is that you?" Addy's amazed voice came back.

"Yes, it's me. Now find something to stand on so you can climb out of this hole."

There was only a slight pause before Harry heard something moving in the hut. He had prayed that there would be something in there for her to climb on. He wasn't ready to risk taking her out the door of the hut if she could get out through the hole. He turned his attention to moving an old barrel from behind the hut. Once under the hole, it should be just the right height for Addy to climb on.

The barrel was in place when a loud voice made Harry freeze. "Get on out there and guard that girl, Barrett."

Someone, probably Uncle Marty, had finally realized that his hostage was unguarded. Harry leaned on the barrel and listened. They had been so close. Had Addy heard the order? There was nothing but quiet from inside the hut, so she must have heard the voice.

Next Harry heard a scraping as if someone were striking a match. Barrett must be lighting a cigarette. Soon a tuneless humming began. Not pleasant to the ears, but it might mask the noise Addy was bound to make on the way out. Harry pulled himself up on the barrel, and just as he peered in the hole, Addy peeked out. Her face looked dirty even in the dim light, but her smile was brilliant. He motioned for her to climb through the hole and reached for her arms to help. The stones around the opening seemed fairly tight. Addy struggled with her dress. This was one time Harry would have agreed that she should wear her skirts stylishly short.

She was almost out when the worst happened. A stone broke loose from the edge and tumbled down over the wall and the barrel and clattered to the ground.

"What's that?" Barrett yelled.

"Come on," Harry said and pulled Addy onto the barrel. "We'll run for it." They scrambled down from the barrel, turned, and came face to face with Barrett, who stood at the corner of the hut.

They looked at each other for what seemed like a long time. Finally Barrett turned abruptly without a word and went back to the front of the hut. Harry grabbed Addy's arm. "Let's go." The cousins ran across the clearing to the woods and stopped.

Someone yelled from in front of the shed. "What's going on over there, Barrett?"

"Nothing that I know of," Barrett answered. "Maybe a rock fell off the hut."

"Well, check the girl." Harry heard grumbling as footsteps approached the hut.

"He's not telling," Harry whispered to Addy, "but they'll see you're gone. Let's get out of here."

"Shouldn't we go through the woods?" Addy asked as Harry steered her forward. "They'll catch up to us if we stay out in the open."

"We might get lost in the woods," Harry said. "Besides, we have a vehicle, and they don't."

Addy gave him a puzzled look but followed as he retraced his earlier path. It seemed to Harry like a million years had passed since he'd come this way in the afternoon. It was hard to see where to walk in the dark, but Harry hurried Addy on, determined to put as much distance as possible between them and the bootleggers.

Shouts sounded from the clearing. Addy's absence had been discovered.

"How could you let that girl get away?" Uncle Marty yelled. "Why can't anything get done right around here? Well, don't just stand there. Find her! She can't be far away."

Harry glanced back as he ran. White shapes that must be the bootleggers' white shirts darted across the clearing. He realized that the moon must have risen when he wasn't watching. The moonlight reflected brightly off Addy's yellow dress, dirty as it was. Before he could steer her deeper into the woods, a yell went up.

"Over here. I see someone over here." It sounded like Joe-Joe. Soon, running footsteps pounded across the meadow toward the cousins.

"Uh-oh," Harry said. "Better turn on the speed."

In a final burst of energy, the pair reached the creek and clambered through the ditches and shallow water. The motorcycle sat where Harry had left it, ready for a quick get-away. "Get on," he yelled at Addy as he hit the starter. She climbed on the second seat and clutched his middle.

It took Harry a couple tries before the cycle roared to life. As they lurched off the stand, hands reached out. It was Joe-Joe, and the murderous look on his face showed that he meant business. He grabbed Addy's arm, but she screamed and gave him a mighty shove. Caught off balance, the man stumbled back.

That brief moment gave Harry all the time he needed. He twisted the throttle, and the cycle shot forward. With no reason to stay hidden, Harry steered into the open meadow. Joe-Joe was chasing them, but it was clearly a doomed effort. When Harry looked back, the man had stopped to shake his fist at them.

"Won't they come after us in the car?" Addy yelled in Harry's ear.

"Oh, no, they won't be doing that any time soon," Harry said and grinned back at Addy.

"Why not?"

Harry slowed down as they reached the opening to the lane. He put his foot down and stopped. He turned to look across the meadow to the clearing. Lanterns twinkled like lightning bugs back there. Of course, he couldn't hear what was being said, but he had an idea that it wasn't fit for decent ears.

"Why not?" Addy repeated.

"I guess you could say that I fixed their cars," Harry replied. "And the plane, too, for that matter. A car has to have gas and a plane has to have spark plug wires to run. They have neither."

"Too bad," Addy said. "Can we go home now?"

"That's a terrific idea, cousin. Let's do it." Harry pushed off again, and in a few minutes they were almost to the airfield and safety.

CHAPTER 13

Ernie Comes Through

The airfield was dark and deserted when they arrived. Harry felt a brief surge of disappointment because he was anxious to talk to Ernie and explain his disappearance. His boss must have been mystified when Harry didn't show up to be introduced to Lindbergh.

"We should stop here and call the police and our parents," Harry yelled back to Addy, "but it looks like the terminal building is locked. Maybe I could get in through a window."

"Please, let's go home," Addy said. "I just want to go home."

"Then that's what we'll do." The bootleggers would have at least a forty-five minute walk before they could get to a telephone. That should be plenty of time to get home and call the police to catch the crooks.

Addy's house blazed with light from every window when the cousins roared up. Harry was glad to see his father's car parked at the curb in front. In seconds the porch and yard were filled with their families and friends and neighbors, who hugged the pair while laughing and, in the case of Mother and Aunt Esther, crying. Harry saw Ernie's smiling face on the porch, and Nate and Violet rushed across the yard. A babble of questions and demands for explanation rose from the group.

Harry held up a hand. "We'll tell you all about it, but first I need to call the police so they can catch some bootleggers who kidnapped Addy."

Several people gasped, and Addy's mother looked like she needed a place to sit down. Mother led Aunt Esther and Addy back up the porch steps and into the house.

"The police are here," Father said. "Where is that sergeant?"

"Right here, sir." A uniformed policeman stepped forward from the porch.

Harry explained the situation quickly, and the policeman ran inside the house to call the station before jumping in his car to speed away. He seemed confident that the bootleggers would be spending the night in jail.

Ernie walked up to Harry and shook his hand. "I'm glad you're safe, and I'm proud of you."

"I'm sorry about missing Lindbergh," Harry said.

"Not a problem," Ernie said and placed his hand on Harry's shoulder. "There were more important things to consider today."

Ernie left, and other friends and neighbors shook hands and went home as well. The families moved to the kitchen, where Addy and Harry sat down to eat a late dinner. Harry was starved, but he hadn't noticed until the smell of leftover fried chicken reminded him. The cousins told their stories while they ate.

Harry heard for the first time how Addy had gone to Barrett's house to ask him what he was doing at the airfield in the middle of the night. While she was there, Joe-Joe and Hank had arrived and accidentally spilled the beans in front of her about the expected evening shipment. Barrett tried to convince them to leave her behind, but they wouldn't hear of it.

"Where was Susan?" Aunt Esther asked. "I thought you went over there to visit her. That's why we didn't worry until this evening."

"She was gone. Sent back to Chicago," Addy said and picked up another biscuit. "They were closing down their operation here. I heard Joe-Joe say that the federal agents had gotten way too nosy."

"I can't believe all of this took place right under our noses," Aunt Esther said.

"That's how this bootlegging business operates," Uncle Erik said. "Marty owned businesses that were probably only fronts for his real money-maker, bootlegging illegal moonshine and whiskey."

An hour later the Allertons picked up Fred, who was

about to fall asleep standing up, and started for home. Harry would follow on his cycle. The police had just called to say that they had caught the crooks. There would still be questions by the dozens, but for now everyone was satisfied.

Addy followed Harry out onto the porch. Uncle Erik and Aunt Esther had hugged and thanked him repeatedly for saving Addy, and now they left the cousins alone.

"What do you think will happen to Barrett?" Addy asked. She still wore the stained and dirty yellow dress. Her face was clean, but her short hair poked out every which way.

Harry sighed. "I'm not sure."

"He did help us escape," Addy said and looked away.

"You can be sure I'll tell the police that, but Addy. . ." He hesitated.

"I know," Addy interrupted him. "You don't have to say it. Barrett was the wrong friend for me from the start. I should have listened to you."

Harry remained silent.

"Even so, I don't want him to go to jail." Addy walked over to the porch railing and turned her face up to the night sky. The moon was overhead and cast a bright glow over the front yard. "I'm sorry, Harry. Can you ever forgive me? I know you tried to help, but I've been so mixed up lately."

"You're forgiven. I'm not sure I did such a good job of helping," Harry admitted. "I knew something wasn't right with Uncle Marty and his gang, but I didn't tell anyone else. If I had, you might not have been kidnapped. You'd been madder than a hornet, but you would have been safe. I'm sorry, too."

140

"It's okay, Harry. I chose to lie to my parents and dis-
obey them. They'll punish me because I lied to them, but
they'll forgive me, too," Addy said. "Do you think God
will forgive me? I've been so awful to everyone lately.
God must be really mad at me."

"My mother says that God doesn't hold grudges the
way people seem to. He gets sorrowful instead. And she
says He forgives in a blink of an eye, if we ask Him."
Harry moved closer to Addy.

Addy grinned at him. "Then that's what I'll do." She
put her arms around her cousin and hugged him. "Thanks,
Harry. Thanks for everything."

"It was my pleasure," Harry said, and he meant it.

The telephone rang early Wednesday morning. Ernie
asked Harry to come out to the airfield to help him.
Harry's head felt fuzzy with fatigue, but he dressed and
started for Wold-Chamberlain. An early morning rain
shower had washed the dust off everything and left a
fresh smell in the air.

The bright cool morning cleared his head, but that
only led him to think about yesterday. Now that Addy
was safe, he let himself think about Charles Lindbergh
and the missed visit. It was disappointing, but perhaps he
would get another chance someday to meet the famous
aviator. Now that Addy was back on the right track, he
intended to find a way to fly again. He was determined to
do it, even if he got so airsick he turned green. Ernie said
it would pass, and Harry was counting on that.

There were many more cars at the airfield than was

normal for a Wednesday morning. Harry looked around with interest as he parked his cycle. He went through the hangar to the shop and grabbed his apron. Oddly, there wasn't an airplane waiting for service. He wondered why Ernie needed him. Maybe there were extra flights coming in soon. Where was his boss, anyhow?

Laughter and voices came from another hangar across the way. Harry walked out front to look in that direction.

"Harry! Come over here," Ernie called, and Harry ran to obey.

Several men stood around an airplane that Harry didn't recognize. All of them were dressed in suits except Ernie and one other tall, brown-haired man. He wore a leather jacket and knickers and looked familiar to Harry.

"I want you to meet a friend of mine," Ernie said and turned to the tall man. "Charlie, this is the mechanic I've been telling you about. Mechanic turned bootlegger catcher, I should say. Harry Allerton, meet Charles Lindbergh."

Harry stood dumbstruck until Mr. Lindbergh stuck out his hand. "Pleased to meet you, Harry. I heard you had an exciting day yesterday."

Still Harry could only nod, shake hands, and grin. Mr. Lindbergh looked so much younger than he expected. Why, he didn't look any older than Harry's brother Larry, yet he had flown across the Atlantic Ocean all by himself.

Finally Harry found his voice long enough to talk to Mr. Lindbergh, who seemed more interested in hearing about Harry's adventures with the bootleggers than talking about himself and his flight.

After awhile, it was time to push Lindbergh's plane

out to the taxiway. He was due at the next stop on his tour by afternoon. Harry observed as the pilot carefully checked each part of his plane. At last he shook hands with everyone and climbed aboard.

"Harry," Mr. Lindbergh called. Harry ran up close to the small cockpit window. "I'll expect to see you up here with me some day soon." With that, the pilot waved and revved his engine.

Harry watched as the small plane lifted into the sky. The others walked back to the terminal building, but Harry never took his eyes off the speck that was Lindbergh's airplane. In a minute he realized that the plane had banked sharply to the left. It was coming back. Was something wrong? He shaded his eyes with his hands and peered up. Everything looked fine, and the engine sounded normal.

The plane circled and swooped low over the runway. Just as it went over Harry's head, the wings gave an unmistakable wiggle. Harry laughed and waved broadly. Lindbergh had given him the pilot's salute. The *Spirit of St. Louis* soared back up and disappeared behind a fluffy white cloud.

Harry listened until the only sound was a bird scolding a squirrel on the roof of the terminal building. It was time for life to get back to normal, he thought, but couldn't help remembering that Ernie had said normal changes sometimes. That was just fine if airplanes and flying could stay part of his life.

There's More!

The American Adventure continues with *Black Tuesday*. Alice Harrington and her cousin Fred Allerton are about to see their lives changed. First their cousin Addy develops a cough that won't go away. Fred's father, a doctor, is worried that Addy may have tuberculosis and will have to go away to a sanatorium. She may even die.

Then the stock market crashes on what people call Black Tuesday. Alice and Fred don't understand what the fuss is about, but it's obvious their parents are worried. People are losing their jobs, and some of the richest children at school are having to move out of their beautiful homes.

What can Alice and Fred do to help Addy and their friends? And will the financial problems cause them to lose their homes, too?